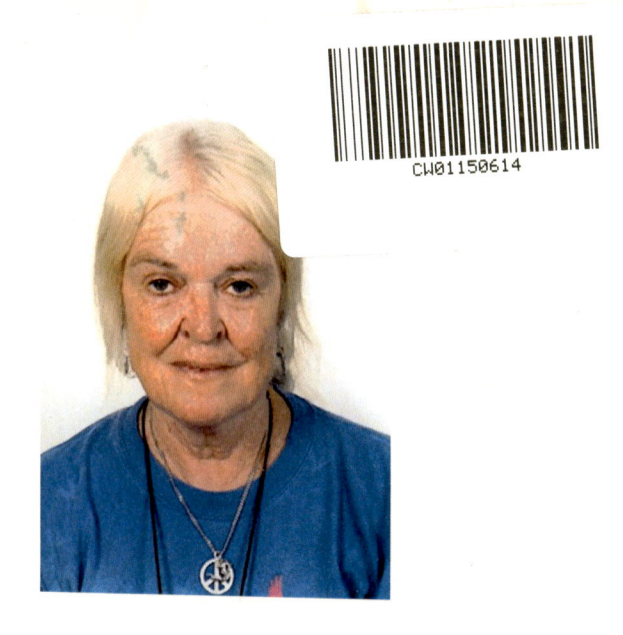

About the Author

I have a first degree in History and Theology and a PhD in Comparative Religion. I first became aware of Olympe de Gouges when I was studying for my first degree; I was amazed by the radically feminist views expressed by this humbly born woman in eighteenth century France. I wanted to give a 'voice' to this little known woman who clearly possessed great beauty, intelligence and independence of mind. The writing of Olympe de Gouges was revolutionary but her personal life is little known. The 'gaps' in the historical knowledge gave rise to the possibilities for the creation of a novel.

Marie and the Judgement of Paris

Heather Meacock

Marie and the Judgement of Paris

Olympia Publishers
London

www.olympiapublishers.com
OLYMPIA PAPERBACK EDITION

Copyright © Heather Meacock 2019

The right of Heather Meacock to be identified as author of this work has been asserted in accordance with sections 77 and 78 of the Copyright, Designs and Patents Act 1988.

All Rights Reserved

No reproduction, copy or transmission of this publication may be made without written permission. No paragraph of this publication may be reproduced, copied or transmitted save with the written permission of the publisher, or in accordance with the provisions of the Copyright Act 1956 (as amended).

Any person who commits any unauthorised act in relation to this publication may be liable to criminal prosecution and civil claims for damage.

A CIP catalogue record for this title is available from the British Library.

ISBN: 978-1-78830-401-6

'This is a work of historical fiction; Olympe de Gouges (Marie Gouze) was a real person who lived during the period of the French Revolution. Her relationships with Mirabeau and with the disaffected priest, Father Michel, are entirely the products of the writer's imagination.

First Published in 2019

**Olympia Publishers
60 Cannon Street
London
EC4N 6NP**
Printed in Great Britain

Dedication

I dedicate this novel to my beloved grandchildren, Issy, Becca, Thomas and Sebby

Acknowledgements

I would like to thank my friend, Sylvia Millam, for her advice and first typing of the manuscript of this novel.

Part One

1755 Childhood

Marie Gouze sat cross-legged by the gate of the meadow, her thin shift pulled up over her knees, making a pillow in her lap for the week-old calf. She tickled the inside of its ear with a long grass, then removed it and chewed the end. With her other hand, she traced patterns in the dust. The air of the Languedoc meadow was stagnant with the foetid smell of cow dung and the heat of August 1755. The upper pastures were brown and scorched, in the distance the herd stood dolefully. The cows had abandoned their search for fresh grass and now followed the shade of the few trees in circular motion, bovine sundials. At midday the landscape lay as if in torpor. Nothing moved except the flies, performing their desultory dance around the beasts' heads, droning heavily.

    Marie left off chewing and, gathering together a bundle of grasses, swished them gently over the calf, to save him from the torment of the flies. How like the dandelion seed, she thought, was the soft hair inside his ear. From the house in the village below the meadow she heard, faintly, the call of her mother, summoning her home. She ignored it. She would stay yet awhile, though the heat was oppressive and her flaxen hair clung in damp strands down her narrow back. She had come to the meadow to escape the misery of her home. Shifting the calf's head she lay back on the prickly grass and wriggled luxuriously, screwing up her eyes against the relentless sun.

Behind her shut eyelids a warm red light glowed. She let herself imagine the beginning of the world, which the old priest had told her about, when strange animals had lived and when a man called Noah had saved them from the flood. She would like to have lived in this world filled with animals, who, it was said, went into the Ark two by two. It sounded very orderly; they belonged to each other. In her world it was difficult to know where one belonged. She drifted into sleep.

Marie was fatherless. Her father, Pierre Gouze, had been a butcher. He had died when she was only two years old, so she did not remember him. But she thought she could remember the smell of blood from the abattoir and the sound of the axe clunking with dull thuds into the sides of the cows, portioning the carcases for the market. When she was six years old she remembered passing the butcher's shop in the nearby town of Montauban. She had seen a dead calf on the block, its bags and tubes scattered in disarray beside it. Inside the meat shed lay rows of dead calves, shrouded like corpses in white cloths, which allowed only their sawn-off, bleeding stumps to be seen. There were whole sheep waiting to be dismembered, piled in a heap, their wool mangled and blood stained. Dim eyes peered brainlessly from narrow, elongated heads. Whole pigs were suspended in rows, their gaping innards exposed. Grinning, rubbery pigs' heads lay in a trough on the floor. She had never forgotten this fearful sight, though it was two years ago, and, since then, she had always avoided the butcher's shop. Marie loved all animals. She could not regret her father's death, since he had been a butcher. It was shameful, degrading, to be the daughter of such a man.

When she was four, her mother, born Anne Olympe

Mouisset, had married a member of the police, Dominique-Raymond Cassaigneau. But her step-father showed little interest in her, except to chastise her. There was another man, she vaguely remembered, who had petted and caressed her when she was very small. But then he had gone away. She seemed to remember that he wore fine clothes and smelled sweetly, but she could not really recall his face. Her youthful experience had led her to distrust men.

The family lived in the village of Pont d'Herault, a short distance from Montauban. As members of the bourgeoisie they were poor, but not exceptionally so by the standards of rural France in 1755. Her mother had not married wisely, for a girl who descended from the prosperous Mouisset family. She was the mother of a son and two girls by her first marriage and another son already, by this present union. She expected, of course, to bear yet more children. Marie was the younger daughter of her first marriage, born on May 7, 1748. Anne's features still bore traces of the charms of her youth, now much faded with child-rearing and poverty, after two feckless marriages. But she was still hopeful by disposition and, since her instinctive plan for overcoming her endless labours was to leave them until tomorrow, she managed to live in slatternly cheerfulness. Still, the dilatory habits of her daughter were enough to try any woman. She went to the door of the police house and called again to her daughter. Would the child ever return and lend a hand with the wringing of the clothes? This was a task hardly to be undertaken by a woman with a baby at the breast. In the meadow above, Marie was almost out of earshot and her mother could scarcely follow her there, exposing her nakedness to the eyes of the villagers. So she reasoned, although this year of 1755 was not one of prudishness, living as they did in the ever present stench of birth and death, animal and human. In truth it was the heat and her natural inertia which prevented the mother from pursuing her errant daughter. So she continued suckling the child, crooning tunelessly and occasionally shifting it to her other arm to give the *daube* a stir, lest its bloody thickness should cause it to burn. Her husband was a hungry man, lusty with the appetite of a man who worked hard. He would be hungry when he returned home, in every way, and it would not have occurred to his wife to deny him.

In the meadow, Marie woke with a start; an unexpected noise had stirred her consciousness. She blinked and instinctively pulled down her dress as she sat up, disturbing the calf. In protest at such a sudden awakening, it staggered to its spindly legs and lolloped across the grass in search of its natural mother. Marie's noonday sleep had been disturbed by the Marquis Lefranc de Pompignan, a local nobleman whose estates were extensive in this part of Languedoc. He halted his grey mare on the path beside the gate to the meadow and called to the child;

'*Mon enfant!* Why are you sleeping thus in the midday sun? Get up and go about your work!'

Marie rose and bobbed an angular curtsey; she had been taught to respect and fear the nobility. Monsieur Le Marquis she knew by sight and in her eyes he was an awesome figure. Marie, though considered 'odd' among the girls of the village, especially for her unaccountable love of animals, had nevertheless an ordinary girl's love of finery. She stole a covetous glance at the frothy lace billowing at the marquis' fleshy throat and then to the grey silk of the doublet enveloping his broad torso. Her eyes went to the sheathed sword by his side, the traditional mark of the nobility. Irrelevantly, she wondered whether it ever performed the same task as her real father's meat cleaver had done, on animals or on people?

The marquis swung his leg over the horse and dismounted.

'Hold my horse,' he commanded abruptly. Obediently she took the bridle, while the marquis strode a pace or two away and opened his breeches to relieve himself, not bothering to get out of the eyeshot of the child. He sauntered back, adjusting his clothing, and took her small face in his hand, scrutinizing it with bold, lascivious eyes.

'You are the daughter of Anne Gouze, she who was once married to the butcher, are you not?'

'Yes, Monsieur Le Marquis.'

'And how old are you, child?'

'Eight sir, that is, I shall be eight on my feast day next Spring.'

'Hmm,' replied the nobleman, musingly. As if to himself he continued, 'You have a look of your mother, though it is hard to say yet whether you will equal her in beauty. Though I dare say it has gone off her now. Women's beauty fades fast.'

Marie scarcely knew how to answer, nor indeed did it seem that any was expected. Still the nobleman held her face in his grasp. His long tapering fingers were vice-like in their grip as they pinched the delicate bones of her jaw, and his breath upon her smelt stalely of wine and garlic as he peered more closely into her large innocent eyes, noting the peony mouth and the transparent white skin. Suddenly he laughed coarsely;

'A real little bud for the picking you will be, *ma petite*, soon, when you've filled out a little. Now be off home with you.' So saying, he turned and planted a gentle kick at Marie's small rump with his spurred boot, before fitting it securely in the stirrup and hoisting his bulk on to the grey mare's back. With a clap of his legs, he urged the mare forwards and was gone.

Marie descended slowly and reluctantly to the house, thinking, this time, not of her calf but of that froth of lace at the throat of the Marquis Lefranc de Pompignan, and how she would love a little, just a little, to trim the coarse white cotton robe her mother was stitching for her first Holy Communion this coming harvest-time. She was lost in a reverie of billowing lace and crackling white satin when her father returned from his work. He disliked the child, who was not of his flesh. She irritated him perpetually with her finicky ways, her perpetual desire to wash herself. In this year of 1755, baths were rarely taken and water was regarded with suspicion, as weakening the constitution. There was something odd and unnatural about Marie, he thought.

'I suppose you have been away skulking in the meadow again with your pretty calves?' he growled. 'You are a lazy child. You give yourself airs, as if you are of the aristocracy, not the bourgeoisie. You should remember your station in life and give help to your mother with the cooking of the *daube*.'

'Father, I do not care to smell the flesh of animals cooking, or to eat meat,' she replied, defiantly.

For this response she received a stinging blow on her cheek from Dominique Cassaigneau. He was a police officer who knew the worth of a blow or two, where recalcitrant children were concerned. There was nothing unusual, in Marie's experience, about such a demonstration of paternal affection, she had no expectation of anything different from men. What was unusual was the growing knot of rebellion she felt. Nevertheless, she dutifully helped her mother, for she was much attached to her, and, young though she was, she understood enough to pity her life of perpetual childbearing and domestic drudgery.

Later that evening, Monsieur Cassaigneau lay slumped in exhaustion before the fire, his legs spread-eagled, his boots upturned, exposing the mud encrusted on their soles. He snored rhythmically. Marie sat by the window and put her face to the slit, to cool her cheek. She peered into the gloom. There had been another blow at supper time when her father caught her surreptitiously swallowing her bread dry and tipping her portion of the stew onto her mother's plate.

'*Maman,*' said Marie.

'Hmm,' answered her mother, abstractedly. For once she was industriously occupied, stitching the child's dress for Holy Communion, for the event was only a week away, and nothing yet ready.

'Why is it some girls will have pretty things to wear in the church this coming Sunday, and I will not?'

'Foolish child, you know the reason well enough. Some are rich and some are poor. 'Tis the way God wills it. It is not for us to question the will of the Almighty.' She shrugged indifferently.

'I saw the Marquis Lefranc de Pompignan this afternoon when I was in the meadow. He looked very fine in silk and lace,' mused her daughter.

'Well, he is a nobleman, Marie, you know that.' She smiled. 'What would you expect? A fine, comely gentleman like the marquis would surely look well.'

'I detest him!' cried the child, thinking of his grip on her chin, his face leering into hers.

'Marie, for shame!' exclaimed her mother, surprised out of her usual languid demeanour. 'Do not say such things... you of all people. It's wicked.'

'Why may I not say so, Maman. Why is it wicked if it is true? Why especially for me?'

Madame Cassaigneau looked closely at her daughter and then, as if seeming to make up her mind, put down her stitching before she replied.

'Come close, close here, my daughter. Put you ear to my mouth.' Marie obeyed, puzzled.

'He is your father. The marquis is your father.' Marie gazed at her mother, blankly. The words had no meaning for her.

'Maman, you live here, with Papa and me and the other children. You know you do. What can you possibly mean? You live with us.'

'Live? What has 'live' got to say to anything?' laughed her mother. 'Monseigneur, the marquis, is your *father*, I say.'

Still, complete blankness from the child. The truth of her ignorance dawned on Madame Cassaigneau. She rested her hands on her hips and laughed uproariously, rocking backwards and forwards on her heels, only smothering her laughter at the warning grunts of wakefulness which came from her sleeping husband. To think of all the time this child spent mooning about with animals, yet had not made the simple connection between copulation and the procreative function.

'Listen you little silly. Do you not know what makes babies? You've seen the bulls mounting the cows often enough. That's what makes the calves you love so well, not *living together!* Do you see Madame and Monsieur Vache playing house together?' Her own mirth overcame her and she laughed aloud again. 'You silly girl. Monsieur Le Marquis is your father because of what we did together.'

Marie was appalled. To think of her mother, anyone, doing that! She had of course seen animals mating in the fields, but had thought of it, if she had thought at all, as a bullying game played by the male upon a patient, resigned female. It was all too true, as her mother had surmised, that she had not connected the act of copulation with the resulting offspring.

'Did you really do that, mother? But why? Why?'

'Because men like it, I suppose.' Madame Cassaigneau laughed again. 'And it's not 'did' but 'do', still do. That is why you have your brothers and sister, and yet more to come, I'll swear.'

Marie turned this amazing information over in her mind, then, as if to impress it clearly upon her understanding, she repeated,

'You did this with Monsieur Le Marquis, and that is why he is my father?'

'Yes,' replied her mother, with some asperity, for she was becoming impatient with the child's incredulity. 'And there is no need to sound so shocked, my girl. Why, with a nobleman such as he is, it was an honour. Not every woman is chosen in such a way. He said… I remember his very words, "I was a bud ripe for the picking." A pretty expression. A fine gentleman.' Madame Cassaigneau shrugged, and as if throwing off pleasant memories and returning to indifferent reality, she continued, flatly, 'I was already married to Pierre Gouze. He knew he was not your father. It was well known that Lefranc de Pompignan had loved me since I was a girl. But a woman needs a legal father for her children and Pierre Gouze was well paid for his silence. He died early. You were barely two years old. So then I was married again, to Dominique-Raymond, and taught you to call him "father".

This was a great deal for Marie to take in.

'So Pierre Gouze, the butcher, was not my father?'

'No, indeed.' Madame Cassaigneau laughed. 'They say it is a rare person who knows their own father. Only a mother really knows, and then, not always.'

'Why does my real father not own me?' asked Marie, in great wonder at these revelations.

'How could he do so? When you were very small he showed great affection for you, my Marie. He would have taken you from me, and proposed that I should leave you to his care, to educate you. But I could not bear to part with you. I was already married to another man. Jean-Jacques Lefranc de Pompignan was in the past. We had lost the moment of our young love, you might say. We had gone our separate ways. Time passed. As time went on, Lefranc de Pompignan could no longer acknowledge you. Besides, they say he is a man of letters, a scholar as well as a nobleman. I would not really know, but I know he has more to do than think of a little by-blow child.'

Marie returned to the window, staring into the gloom. Her mother had told her that her true father did not recognise her. He was a nobleman and well educated. He could teach her to read and give her fine clothes, all the advantages she craved. Instead he chose to treat her with scorn. "A bud ripe for the picking". Those had been his very words this afternoon. She hated him. Never, never, would she be treated in such a way as the bull treated the cow. She never thought to blame her mother, who, according to her own words, had refused her father's help when she was a small baby. Something in her mother's manner, her placid acceptance of the lot of women, her pride, even, made Marie feel it would be useless, unkind, to speak to her of her feelings. We are all of us ultimately alone and she recognised this, instinctively. So she simply said,

'And the lace mother? I suppose there is no chance of a little lace?' Nothing, not even the revelations of this conversation, quite extinguished her girlish obsession with finery.

'My child, since your heart is set on it, I will steal a bit from my best camisole!'

Marie turned and hugged her mother. A sudden thought came to her. She coloured with vicarious shame, though there was no fear her mother would see the red of her cheeks in the dim evening light, 'Mother, have you ever told anyone else what... what you have just told me?'

Madame Cassaigneau smiled and replied, 'Only the priest, of course. One has to tell the priest, in confession. Poor Father Francis, I fear I shocked him eight years ago at confession. Poor dried out old stick that he was! Perhaps I brought him to an early death!' She chuckled and poked her daughter playfully in the ribs.

'What will you have to say, my pretty daughter, to fine young Father Michel, at your First Confession?'

1755 Father Michel

The village of Pont d'Herault near Montauban lay in two parts, "La Place" below, and, reached by a winding narrow track up the hill, "L'Eglise", above. Most of the inhabitants lived at "La Place"; there was a motley collection of some forty straggling cottages, rotten with poverty, their malignant walls bulging ominously. These were strung along a narrow lane, it could scarcely be called a road. There they lay, miserable, grim buildings, black with poverty, drunken mounds in the light of the August morning. It was six o'clock and the opaque sky already promised another sweltering day. The only living creature in sight was a mangy dog, barking at the end of a rusty chain, tethered at the end of the lane.

    The church of Mary Queen of Sorrows stood two kilometres distant, stark against the sky at the top of the hill. The Romanesque tower of the church rose black and sphinx-like, silhouetted against the horizon. A worn, deeply indented cattle grid separated this bastion of spirituality from the dung of the world of men and beasts. Inside, the darkness of the narrow building was penetrated only by the rays of light shining through the stained glass window behind the altar, a lurid splash of red and yellow, depicting the Passion of Christ in bloody realism. His head was flung back and his body was twisted in the contortions of death. His side was ripped open and bleeding. His feet were like claws nailed together on the cross. Before the altar table, spread in pristine white, knelt Father Michel Dupre, curate of the village of Pont d'Herault and surrounding districts. He was celebrating early Mass, served only by Adolphe, a boy from the village. Father Michel spread wide his arms in a gesture which embraced the faithful of the empty church and the whole world.

'*Dominus vobiscum,*' he intoned, genuflecting deeply. Carefully, with a rapt expression indispensable to the ritual, he continued his performance. Father Michel's performance was immaculate, his gestures like those of a ballet dancer. His handsome, ascetic face took on an expression of total withdrawal from the world as he lifted the wafer aloft and broke it according to the explicit instructions of his God. He let one small piece of the wafer fall into the wine, signifying the union of body and blood which, by his hands, and through his office, he was about to make with the God of Abraham. Delicately, he brushed one minute crumb from his long, tapering fingers into the chalice, in fastidious care that no part of God should fail to be consumed. In clear, pure tones he recited the *Agneus Dei*; in rapture he drank the brew which was now the substance of He who was represented bleeding in the stained-glass window. The magic was complete; Father Michel ate and drank in ecstasy.

He was a very young priest, only twenty years of age, but he was already addicted to the daily dose of the drug which was the Mass. He was invigorated and renewed by his spiritual orgasm. He performed the ablutions, wiping the sacred vessels with infinite care, to ensure no contamination should come into contact with the sacred elements. He withdrew from the main altar and entered the chapel devoted to the Virgin Mary.

There stood a plaster statue, about four feet high, depicting the Mother of God. Her china-blue eyes smiled at him kindly. She was his good friend, his protector and loved one. Father Michel was oblivious of the simpering anonymity of the faceless statue, he did not see the chips and cracks in the plaster folds of the blue robe which covered her chastely from neck to feet. He was enchanted by the doll's face and reached out his hand to touch the icy-white cheek. Nothing, not even his love for her Son, compared with his devotion to the Virgin. She epitomised all that was serene and pure in womanhood, he cherished her chastity dearly. Kneeling in prayer, Father Michel addressed her reverently, yet intimately.

'Dearest Mary, help and guide me. Be with me every minute of the day and stay with me at night. I need your love.' His prayers were natural and intimate, quite different from the prescribed Latin formula he used for addressing God. He lifted his gaze to her in simple, blind adoration. So absorbed was he in talking to the statue, that he did not hear the approach of his elderly housekeeper. She had come quietly into the church and tapped him gently on the shoulder.

'Excuse me Your Reverence, but the children are here, as expected. That is, they've come to be confessed.'

Father Michel rose, slowly and reverently and made the sign of the cross before the statue, before turning to his housekeeper. He had forgotten his appointment to hear the confessions of the children due to receive Holy Communion for the first time this coming Sunday, the Feast of Corpus Christi. There were seven of them, a bedraggled little band, who eyed their spiritual leader with a mixture of apprehension and frank curiosity. Father Michel was, truth to tell, irritated by this interruption to his devotions, nevertheless, his views on the sacraments were rigidly correct. He would have tramped ten kilometres through the snow to baptise a dying child and would have been appalled at the idea of these children receiving the sacrament in a state of sin. That children such as these could be sinners, he had no doubt. You had only to look at them, children of the soil that they were, destined for mindless fornication like the animals they tended. The children of Pont d'Herault matured early; more often than not, girls coming to the church to marry, would precede the event by lying in the cornfields with one or several lusty young lads, only consenting to put up the banns when they were with child. He regarded the children sternly, and without speaking, motioned them to sit on the benches. Taking his stole, he entered the confession box.

One by one the children whispered their misdemeanours to the priest through the grating. They confessed that they had been inattentive during Mass, that they had been lazy, or disobedient, or had told lies. Father Michel half listened and murmured, 'Very well, very well, my child.' Then he absolved each of them, in a perfunctory manner. What mattered was his power to forgive their sins, not what the sins were. It was unnecessary to give the matter very much attention, and he closed his eyes as the last child entered, imagining in his mind the pure white face of the Virgin he had been talking to when so rudely interrupted by this routine duty.

'It is a week since my last confession, Father,' whispered Marie. 'In that time I have been lazy and have not helped my mother as I ought around the house and with the younger children. I have been vain, too, and have thought about pretty clothes. And... and I hate the Marquis Lefranc de Pompignan and wish he was dead. And I'm not sorry, Father, because I do hate him,' she concluded, vehemently. Father Michel opened his eyes. What was this child saying?

'Repeat what you said, child.'

'Father, I said I hate the Marquis Lefranc de Pompignan and I can't ask you to forgive me because I'm not sorry and anyway, he has sinned against me.'

For once Father Michel felt he lacked precedence for dealing with this situation in the confession box. Never, since his ordination, had he met with such a defiant and unrepentant sinner. His parishioners, as he well knew, were affably well-disposed towards penitence, although cynically aware of the likelihood of their sinning again and again.

'Come outside and talk to me child,' he said.

Outside the confession box he looked thoughtfully at the small child. She was frail and white, with a mass of fair hair cascading down her back. He took her small hands in his and sat opposite her on the bench, motioning her to sit also. He scrutinized the determined little face without speaking for a moment or two. Then he said, 'What is the trouble, my child? And what is your name?'

'My name is Marie Gouze,' she replied. 'And I have told you what is the trouble. The marquis is my real father, I've discovered from my mother, and he does not own me. He rides around the countryside in fine lace, while I have nothing!' Her lip trembled and, her eyes filling with tears of self-pity, she added passionately, 'It's not *fair!*'

The question of fairness or unfairness was one Father Michel felt ill-equipped to deal with, despite the fact that he had been an exemplary pupil during his time at the seminary. How did one cope with the theological issues raised by the problems of undeserved evil and the disparity of the human lot, in answer to a seven year old child? He was, however, conscious of a rising anger at the behaviour of the nobleman in question. It was typical of the French nobility, ravishing peasant women, leaving them defenceless with the consequences of their actions. It was heedless, arrogant and ungodly. But these were dangerous thoughts, he knew. The church and the nobility were intrinsically linked in eighteenth century France. They acted as mutual props, rotten and decaying buttresses though these were. The church had the monopoly of public worship and immense landed wealth. It was exempt from ordinary taxation, its sole contribution to the treasury was the *don gratuit*. In return it was very useful to the monarchy. The king appointed all bishops and abbots and used this area of patronage to bribe the nobility into political inactivity. All of more than one hundred powerful bishoprics were in the hands of noblemen. Thus the church was deeply divided within itself, between its privileged and unprivileged members, and surely Father Michel himself, curate of this obscure Languedoc village, must count among the most unprivileged of the church's pastors. No, Father Michel had no love for the French nobility.

As he looked at this pure child, he felt enraged that her birth should be due to the disgusting animal behaviour of men such as the Marquis Lefranc de Pompignan. It did not occur to him for a minute to doubt the child's word, for her knew the marquis well. Last summer, while walking in the fields above the church saying his evening office, he had stumbled upon the marquis and a young village girl, probably no more than fourteen years of age. He shuddered with repugnance as he remembered her fat white legs, like great flabby slugs waving in the air, while the marquis swung his leg over as if mounting his mare and pounded away vigorously, as if she had been a lump of dough. The marquis had been amused by the encounter.

'See what you are missing, Father! Take your turn; I'm happy to stand aside for a man of the church!'

How unfathomable were the ways of God; to think that the result of such repulsive acts should be such a child as this. With her doll-like face and china-blue eyes, she reminded him of someone, but his mind could not fathom who that image could be. No, the young priest had no love for the nobility of France. He had heard rumours that some priests, bishops and abbots, acted in the same way as the lecherous nobleman he had surprised in this debased act. Intellectually, Father Michel was a radical. He belonged to the growing number of priests who followed the teachings of Edmond Richer, the seventeenth century canonist who believed the French church should be governed by the whole company of its pastors, not just by powerful archbishops. But emotionally he was an idealist and his devotion to Christ and the Virgin was absolute.

At length, after sitting in silence for some moments, musing upon these matters, Father Michel addressed the child again.

'Listen Marie,' he said, taking both her hands and looking into the depths of her hare-bell eyes, 'you must not let this matter of your birth trouble you so. To be sure, you have been wronged, but so was Our Lord Jesus Christ. Think of it in that way and do not hate, for that is wrong also.' He spoke earnestly, but then his clever, conceptualizer's face broke into a smile.

'And do not think so much of lace and finery, my child. To be sure, you will look very pretty when you receive your first Holy Communion. Very pretty, I say.' He surveyed her thoughtfully, and then continued with renewed passion, 'But Marie, that is not what is important. What is important is that this coming Sunday you will take the Lord Jesus Christ into yourself. He will become part of you. My child, it will be the most wonderful day of your life!'

Marie looked at the priest doubtfully, afraid, almost, of his enthusiasm. She couldn't be quite sure what he meant, about the Lord Jesus being inside her. It sounded queer. She had heard a great deal in the past week, about people being inside other people and she had not liked what she had heard. But at the same time, she liked the young priest, he spoke to her kindly, and looked so much like pictures she had seen of saints. He must of course be right, about the Holy Communion. He must know, being a priest.

'Pray each night, my child. Say, "*Even in the night have I desired thee, Lord. Come, Lord Jesus, come*" — and do not think of that other matter.'

'I will try, Father,' said Marie, smiling shyly.

'Good.' He returned her smile thinking that, reprehensible though the accident of her birth had been, it marked her out from the other village children. She was a finer bred creature.

'Go home to your mother now, Marie. *Au revoir,* until Sunday.'

'*Au revoir,* Father' replied Marie, demurely, dropping a

graceful little curtsey.

Sunday dawned fair. Marie pulled on her new white pantaloons and her stiff white gown of coarse cotton, with the bit of lace at the neck, filched from her mother's best camisole. Everything about her this day was to be white. In her hair was a white camellia, mingling its creaminess with the sheen of her flaxen hair. She picked her way carefully up the hill, lifting her skirts high against the dirt and dust of the lane. She must not be soiled in any way. She felt nervously excited, remembering Father Michel's words. This was to be the most wonderful day of her life. Something unimaginable, miraculous, was going to happen when Jesus was inside her in that little white circle of bread.

During the Mass, Marie tried hard to concentrate, but found her thoughts wandering. How nice the altar looked, with its embroidered white cloth. The smell of incense mingled with that of the sheaf of lilies to the side of the altar rails. Lilies, really, would have been nicer to wear in her hair, than the camellia. Marie recollected her thoughts with a start as she knelt in her place, forcing herself to put aside these vanities. She fixed her eyes on the altar. Her eyes strayed upwards to the great red and yellow splash of the window showing Jesus in his agony. She was glad, so glad, that lay people no longer took the chalice, as Father Michel told her they used to. She did not want to taste the blood of Jesus on her lips. She had tasted blood before, her own blood, when her father struck her and she wrinkled her nose at the memory of the sour taste. Secretly, she had though it a horrid idea, to drink the blood of Our Lord, when she had been told about it in her preparations for Holy Communion. The repellent nature of the communion struck her again, most forcibly, as the bell rang for the *Domina non sum dignus*. With a shock, she recollected where she was, and what was about to happen in just a few minutes. She had been distracted throughout the Mass. How could she go to the altar and receive Jesus with all the others? But her body moved automatically with the rest of the new communicants and she found herself kneeling at the altar rails, her chin lifted, her mouth a little open to receive the host.

Father Michel's eyes strayed to Marie as he deftly distributed the communion to the other children kneeling at the altar rails. How charming she looked in her stiff cotton gown, the flower drooping a little at her ear. Her small mouth was already open, like a little lamb's mouth, pink and soft inside. He could see the little buds on her tongue quite clearly. He moved towards her and placed the host on them.

Marie felt the wafer dissolving on her tongue and waited for something wonderful to happen. Desperately she forced herself to think, *Jesus is actually inside me*. She felt nothing.

1759 Growing Awareness

It was four years later. The corn was still green in the fields above the church of Our Lady of Sorrows on a blustery spring evening in May. The corn undulated, a sea of green waves below a steely-grey sky. The skirts of Father Michel's cassock billowed out as he walked, hand in hand, with Marie around the perimeter of the field, to save damage to the crops. Little had changed in the village of Pont d'Herault during the previous years but Marie had grown in stature and thought the young priest, in beauty. He often thought as he looked at her, kneeling straight and upright, absorbed and serious at Mass, or, as now, laughing and gambolling like a young foal, that with every movement she betrayed the origins of her birth. His feelings about her birth remained ambivalent, for he still hated the nobility as much as it was possible for an earnest and godly young priest to hate. But, without doubt, Marie grew daily finer, rarer, than the young village girls who were her peers.

'Father, will you teach me to read?' Marie asked, suddenly.

This was a surprising request. Very few girls of Marie's generation were literate in rural France in the eighteenth century. Very few people in rural France actually spoke the national language. Marie herself barely spoke French; her native dialect was Occitan, as spoken by the rest of her family and the townspeople of Montauban. He smiled.

'My dear girl, why? Reading will not help you to make your husband a good *daube d'agneau*, when you grow up.'

Marie frowned. She pressed her lips together and answered emphatically, 'Father, I don't intend to have a husband. You know that. I have told you before what I mean to do when I grow up.'

She had walked with him frequently since their first meeting in the confessional before her First Communion. She had told him her fantasy of having a beautiful house in Paris, in a tree lined boulevard. There would be chestnut trees and she had said, 'There will be the rustling of the leaves outside my window. Do you think it is the movement of the leaves, Father, which makes the wind blow?' He had laughed as she had continued, solemnly.

'Inside the house there will be gilt mirrors and satin pillows on my bed. I will live quite alone, except for a young girl to wait on me, but I will not be lonely, for I will have several little dogs to share my bed. They will snuggle up to me as I lie in bed among the fine pillows. I will sit and stroke them and feed them sweetmeats. I will have brightly coloured birds in gilt cages, brought from far off countries. They will sing to me as the sun rises in the morning, as the light streams through the windows. Then the maid will bring me *cafe au lait* and I shall sit on the balcony with the little birds on my shoulder, for they will be tame and I should not like to keep them always in their gilt cage. There will be pink roses entwining the rails of my balcony and I will wear a ruffled morning wrapper, with my hair hanging loose. But later I shall pile it in a fair crown on top of my head with little curls cascading on to my shoulders. For the evening I shall have wonderful flowing gowns, in the shades of the evening sky.'

This vision, impossibly romantic, although worldly, had amused the young priest. Marie was only twelve years old. He knew, as she did not, how fantastically child-like it was, how impossible to realise. There were few alternatives for women at this time, other than marriage. He stole a glance at the child as they walked. Dear God, hasten the day when she will realise the alternative, the only alternative for one as pure and virginal as she. Surely soon she would become aware of it. He envisaged her hair, not piled high in a heap of curls, or, as now, blowing in the evening wind, but shorn from her head, shaved in the beauty of self-denial. A wimple, encasing her perfectly shaped, dome-like skull, would replace the female vanity of her fanciful vision. At length he replied,

'Very well, Marie, I will teach you to read. I have little reading material, aside from the Holy Scriptures, and it is not usual for lay people to read them. But in your case, it will be good for your religious education.'

'Oh Father, I want *any education!* I want to know things! There is so much I want to know, and thank you kindly, dear Father, that you will teach me.'

'Come, Marie. calm yourself. If you would be an educated lady, do not dance around me like the lambs of the field. Walk quietly.'

'Yes, Father,' replied Marie, demurely, though still hardly able to suppress her excitement.

They met each week, and it hard to say which of the pair most relished the meetings, the child or the priest. At first, others in the village regarded these meetings with suspicion. First among the protesters was Marie's stepfather. He remarked that he failed to see the use of the child setting herself up to be a fine lady, but then shrugged and said no more, for in truth his attitude towards the children, particularly this bastard, was one of dour indifference, and the more the child kept out of his way, the better he was pleased. Madame Cassaigneau moaned plaintively at first, for the child was absent on Friday evenings, just at the hour when help with the supper was most needed. However, she too soon shrugged, and then carried on in her habitually languid manner, shifting from one unfinished task to another, a cheerful slattern. Most incensed was Father Michel's housekeeper, Helene, who was fiercely attached to the young priest. She was an ugly, dumpy woman with a slack mouth, above which bristled strong black hairs, an embryo moustache. Generally, she treated the young priest with reverence bordering on adoration; he was the image of the holy picture of St Bernard, hanging on the wall of her cubbyhole of a bedroom. When first she was told of the new arrangements for Friday evenings, she ventured a protest,

'But the young girl will be coming just at the hour of your supper, Father.'

'No matter,' he replied. 'We will share the meal first. Learning on an empty stomach will not be good for the child.' The young priest was quite oblivious of female jealousy.

'There is scarcely enough for yourself alone, Father, what with the price of fish, and the little you can give me for housekeeping out of the miserable stipend you get,' Helene retorted sharply. Father Michel smiled at her.

'The child is a small eater, I have no doubt,' he continued on a note of gentle reproach, 'and I must remind you, Helene, it is not for you, or me either, to question the salary Holy

Church sees fit to give me.'

Father Michel was very aware of the hopeless inadequacy of the stipend which left him nearer to starvation than the majority of the peasants whose spiritual care was entrusted to him. He could not help but be aware. He drank nothing but the poorest quality local wine, a vinegary brew which was despised by many of his parishioners. But he saw nothing ambivalent about the parsimony of a wealthy church towards her pastors and the righteousness of the church. He was a single-minded young man and his thinking was as deep and narrow as the hillside stream which flowed by the church of Our Lady of Sorrows.

The lessons took place in Father Michel's front parlour, a Spartan room ornamented only by a portrait of a simpering Virgin, and bookshelves on which he kept his missal, his breviary, a few theological works from his seminary days and a much-thumbed copy of the New Testament. Marie counted the days between one Friday and the next She always refused the fish which preceded the tuition, confiding her dislike of animal flesh. But she would insist on tossing his salad, carefully mixing the endive and chicory with her small fingers and enquiring solicitously,

'More oil, Father? Have I given you enough vinegar?' Then she would take a leaf or two, tilting back her head before dropping the oily leaves between her lips. She would crumble a morsel of bread and pick at it like a bird as she sat at his feet, while he, fastidiously, separated the fish flesh from the bone with the competence of a surgeon. She delighted to watch him eat. How differently he did so, from her so-called father! And he delighted to watch her. She was his doll, his cherished child.

On Friday evenings, somehow, he did not find time for his soliloquies with the Virgin.

Marie was an apt pupil, with a sparkling, original intelligence. Reading came easily, it was like cracking open a young walnut, one tap and the beautiful fruit was revealed, a miniature brain encased by a protective shell. Her writing, however, was scrawling and laborious, and she found it difficult to spell. Father Michel would watch her little fingers and rounded arms as she struggled to form the letters. How beautiful were the child's arms! He stroked her forearm gently, watching the tiny golden hairs in the evening light. He stroked and stroked, as he spoke to her gently of her childish mistakes.

After a few weeks, Marie began to confront Father Michel with questions about her reading. They had reached the fifth chapter of the Gospel of John. Marie read the text aloud, hesitantly at first and then with increasing confidence.

'Tru...ly, truly I say to you, the Son does nothing of his own ac...cord, accord, yes? But only what he sees the Father doing, for what... ever He does, that the Son does likewise.' She paused and looked up from the book in her lap. 'They must have been very close to each other, Jesus and his father, must they not? I mean, for him to copy his father like that.' She smiled. 'I expect they enjoyed their meals together, as I enjoy mine with you, Father. I hate them at home.' Father Michel tried to explain her mistake, but in doing so he floundered, for she had opened the floodgates of religious difficulty.

'Marie, dear child, you are falling into heresy, although of course you are too young to understand. It has a long name, this mistake of yours. It is called anthropomorphism.' He smiled. 'Imagine trying to spell that, *ma chere!* It means imagining God is a man. But God is not a man, He is Spirit.' Marie frowned.

'If God is not a man, then how can he have a son?' Her small face hardened. 'I know how sons are born, Father. And daughters too. My mother told me about... about Monsieur Le Marquis.' Her cheeks reddened but she continued firmly. 'It's a disgusting thing to do. I thought so then, when she told me, when I was seven. I still think so.'

Father Michel smiled with satisfaction.

'I'm glad you think so, Marie. There is a special reason why I am glad of it, though we will not talk of it now. When you are a little older you will realise for yourself, I pray God. As for your problem now, with God and his Son, I will explain, though you must listen carefully. for it is not easy to understand, even for older and cleverer people than you, my Marie. In a way, you are right. God, not being a man, could not have a son in the ordinary way, for He is also omnipotent, eternal and present in every time and place. We use these words, 'Father', 'Son', because as humans, we are very limited. These are ideas for which we simply do not have the words. They are transcendent ideas. That means,' beyond human knowledge.' He whispered,

'Holy Church has explained for us. Jesus *was God*. We say it in the only way we have to say something so tremendous. And your namesake, Our Lady Mary, was *Theokoleus, the God Bearer.*' Marie dismissed the second part of this disclosure for, in truth, she was not greatly interested in the Mother of God. But she attempted to make sense of the idea that Jesus was God. She failed.

'That's impossible, Father.'

'Why so?'

'Because it makes no sense. It is a...a... what is the word — a contradiction. You have explained many wonderful things about God, that he is in all places and at all times. That he goes on forever and does not die. That he knows everything. No human being is like that and yes, I do see that he cannot be a man. But if that is so, Jesus who *was a man,* cannot also be God. It is like... it is like saying a square is the same thing as a circle.'

Father Michel gazed at her in astonishment. He could not answer. He was perplexed by her thoughts and vaguely aware, in the recesses of his mind, of the child's logic. Because he could not answer her with priestly wisdom he retreated into anger at her lack of faith.

'Marie, it is not for you to set up your ideas against Holy Church. It is for you to believe and to be obedient. Obedience will be absolutely necessary for you in the future that God wants for you.'

Never before had he spoken to her so harshly. Marie was stunned at the rebuke, horrified that she had angered him. 'Yes Father. I am sorry, Father.'

'Sorrow is not enough.' Father Michel rose. Secretly he was pleased by her immediate capitulation, that he had so easily regained mastery over her. His ideas were well-schooled in his priestly duties and he knew what to do.

'We will stop reading now, though in future, remember that you come here to learn and not to ask foolish questions. For now, the time grows late and it is necessary that I hear your confession. For you may expect a long penance, Marie Gouze.'

After she had confessed her want of faith, Father Michel led her outside the church and ordered her to kneel outside his door in the fading evening light, to say her penance. He directed her to kneel where the stones were sharpest, deliberately piling more onto the appointed spot. He lifted the hem of her cotton shift to bare her lower legs before she knelt. Her legs were beautiful, straight, like young saplings. He stared at them, his eyes glowing, then lifted the shift higher to expose the small round globes of her buttocks. Then he let the shift fall. It was, after all, his only chance to save her, to have her as his own. How else could he save her from the squalor of an early marriage? How else could he fit her to become a Bride of Christ? He stood in front of her and looked with satisfaction at the small figure as she knelt, intoning the lengthy prayers he had prescribed for her.

The lessons continued, unchanged in outward harmony. But Marie's behaviour changed without her even knowing it herself. Since early childhood, she had been aware of the isolation of the human soul. She kept some of her questions to herself and took care to pull down her shift closely over her knees.

Marie was now at an age where it was usual for girls to make some contribution to the household budget. She was sent to the Chateau Le Vigin, home of the Duc d'Artagne, some seven kilometres distant, to help in the kitchens. Each morning she would rise before cockcrow and splash cold water from the well into her eyes, before trudging the long distance across fields to the ducal residence. At first she was overwhelmed and excited by the chateau, a great, grey pile, approached by a long drive flanked by tall poplars. But she quickly learned she was not to enter by the great oak door and broad double staircase. She was to go around to the back of the chateau, unseen by anyone. In the servants' quarters, she was to put on a shapeless black dress and an ugly cap, into which she must tuck every strand of her hair. Her task was to scrub floors in the subterranean labyrinth of the kitchen and scullery areas. She would crawl on her hands and knees along endless corridors, driving the scrubbing brush along the stone flags. After an hour her fingers would be wrinkled and bloodless.

Once she was sent to scrub an unfamiliar passage on the ground floor. Still on her hands and knees, she passed an open door. She crept in and gazed in wonder at the elegant green and gold chaises longues and chairs with spindly legs, bowed like children with rickets. The room was cluttered with furniture, but no one was there. The light streamed through the long windows; motes of dust danced in the sunlight which spilled onto the highly polished wooden floor. Marie rose from her knees and took an involuntary step forwards; this was a room such as she would be mistress of one day, except, perhaps, too full and heavy looking. She absentmindedly stroked one of the gold damask cushions; her hands were still numb and she could scarcely feel the softness of the cushion. She shrank back in horror when she saw the wet imprint of her fingers on the cushion, for she should not be there. But, nevertheless, she looked around the room, entranced by all she saw. There were many paintings on the walls, mostly stiff-looking portraits of grand people in fine clothes, wearing haughty expressions. One was very different. It showed a man, looking lustfully at three women who were entirely naked. The women were very beautiful, though perhaps a little overly rounded, to her eyes. One was smiling coyly, another looked angry, while the third had turned her back to expose her powerful buttocks. Looking closely at the title, she saw this painting was called, *Le Bon Jugement de Paris.* Paris, she knew, was the great city in France, where she dreamed of living one day. But she could read the caption beside the painting and it seemed that "Paris" had another meaning, for this was the man's name. He had come to judge which of the three women was the most beautiful. Marie wondered at this. Could it be that all men liked looking at naked women?

She turned from the painting. On the opposite wall, stretching from floor to ceiling, were bookshelves. She had never seen so many books; they made Father Michel's small collection look paltry and insignificant. Hastily drying her hands on her coarse black dress, she approached the shelves and scanned them quickly. She slipped a slim volume inside the front of her dress and looked around furtively, like a hunted black and white magpie. Then she ran from the room, back along the slippery wet stone floors and down to the servants' quarters. In this way, Marie Gouze discovered Voltaire.

The book she had borrowed was in fact a play, called, *Oedipe,* she read that it had first been performed at the Comedie Francaise in 1717, some thirty years before she had been born. The play had created a great scandal, for it had sugested that the Duc d'Orleans, regent after the death of Louis 1V, had seduced his daughter, emulating the sin of Oedipus. Marie read with astonishment;

It is not the son, it is the father:
It is the daughter, not the mother,

> *So far, so good.*
> *They have already produced an Aeteocles*
> *(a son of Oedipus by his mother, Jocasta):*
> *If he were to lose both his eyes,*
> *That would be a story for Sophocles.*

Marie pondered on its meaning as she lay in her bed in the family's house in the village of Pont d'Herault. Could it really be that the father had behaved in such a way to his daughter? She thought of her meeting with the Marquis Lefranc de Pompignan, when she was only seven years old. He had said she was "a bud ripe for the picking". Yes, she believed men could commit such sins but the thought was such an outrage to her mind that she dismissed it at once and thought instead, *how wonderful to write a play, that people would come to see, even people who could not read or write would understand such debauchery and condemn it*! She had heard of many injustices in the world. Father Michel himself had told her that the people in the French colonies in Africa were slaves and were beaten and starved. It could not be right to treat people more cruelly than animals. She resolved that, someday, she would write of such injustices herself.

Several months passed. Borrowing books from the Chateau Le Vigin became a habit with her; she had an insatiable need to read and discover more. She next found another text called *Lettres Philosophiques*. It seemed that Voltaire had found himself in trouble with the authorities in France and had gone to England to study. The trouble, it seemed, was that Voltaire openly criticised the church in France for its despotism and intolerance. Marie read in amazement; she read Voltaire's letters on the Quakers, the Anglicans and the Presbyterians, in England. These people it seemed, followed Christ, but they did so differently. Voltaire had written;

> *This is the land of sects. An Englishman, as a free man, goes to Heaven by whatever route he likes.*

The more she read of the work of Francois-Marie Arouet Voltaire, the more she warmed to his thinking. Especially she liked his letter to the English philosopher, Mr Locke, arguing that animals must have spiritual souls, like humans, for God creates nothing without purpose and he had endowed them with same organs of feeling as those of humans. Marie had long been sure that this was so. Voltaire was a believer, for he had written of Pascal,

"your reasoning would only serve to make atheists were it not that the whole voice of nature cries out that there is a God with a strength as great as the weakness of these subtleties." But he seemed to be a very different kind of believer from those she knew, particularly different from Father Michel. Intuitively, she knew that she would be treading on very dangerous ground, if she told him of her reading. But the habit of confiding in the priest was strong within her, it had been nurtured by him for more than four years. She *must* tell Father Michel; what she had read was so sensible, so *reasonable. She must make him understand!*

She soon had the opportunity to speak to Father Michel, for tomorrow was Friday. During their customary meal of fish and salad she spoke excitedly;

'Father, I have discovered such *interesting reading* in the library of the chateau. Many books and letters by Monsieur Voltaire. He says many surprising things, but I like above all that he believes animals have souls, as we do. He wrote this in a letter to Mr Locke, in England. I have *always* believed that cats and dogs, horses and the young calves have souls, for as Monsieur Voltaire writes, they feel just as we do.' Father Michel dropped his fork in astonishment and said severely,

'Voltaire? You have been reading his pernicious writing? How could you Marie! The man is an infidel, an unbeliever!'

'No, I think not, Father,' replied Marie judiciously. 'I think that Monsieur Diderot may be. I have read some of his works also. One is *Lettre sur les aveugles a l'usage de ceux qui voyent*. Monsieur Voltaire replies to him that the person who is blind should not therefore deny the existence of God. He should, rather, recognise an infinitely capable craftsman who has given many other senses and abilities, besides sight.'

'*These men are atheists, I tell you,*' shouted Father Michel. 'Voltaire and Diderot dare to criticise Holy Church.' Marie thought hard and struggled to answer fairly.

'Yes, I think Monsieur Voltaire does criticise the Church of Rome, but he writes that the English people across the water have many different ways of following Jesus. He does believe in a Supreme Being. I think it is called being a Deist.' Father Michel answered coldly,

'You dare to disbelieve me, a priest of the church! I will argue no further, but will hear your confession, formally. Then you may expect your penance.'

This was as usual. Marie had been given penance many times by Father Michel and had grown used the ritual prayers while she knelt on the stones outside the church. She took it for granted, as a child grows accustomed to every ritual. However, this time, after her confession, Father Michel spoke again.

'This time your penance will be different, Marie. There will be prayers, of course, but afterwards you will remain on your knees. It is my duty to administer flagellation.' Marie hardly knew what this word meant, but, after her prayers she remained kneeling as she had been ordered. She saw from the corner of her eye that the priest had marched purposefully to a willow tree and was carefully examining the branches to find a stick which was both strong and flexible. Then he returned to the kneeling figure. This time he lifted her shift high and draped it carefully over her shoulders, exposing her flanks. In a loud and icy tone he said,

'I warn you, Marie Gouze, that it is my intention to inflict pain upon you. I intend to make you cry out for mercy. It is for the good of your soul. Repeat the words I shall say slowly to you. Then he intoned;

'I... Marie... submit... to... the... teachings... of... Holy... church... and... her... priest.'

With each word, repeated dutifully by the child, he applied the stick, harder each time, systematically and alternately, to each side of her buttocks. Twelve words, twelve cuts. He regarded with satisfaction the pattern of stripes he had made on her buttocks. She had submitted to his will. She was his. But still, it was not enough. The child had not cried out aloud. He intended to make her do so. She must submit absolutely to his will. He continued;

'I see your spirit is stubborn. You shall receive again.

Repeat after me,

'I... suffer... gladly... even... as Our... Lord... Jesus... Christ....has... suffered.'

The pattern of stripes grew and this time, between the words uttered in sobs, Marie's haunches sank to the ground and she cried out to him to stop, please stop. At last he was satisfied. He raised her up and allowed her shift to fall. Then he said,

'You may go now. But, Marie Gouze, do not forget this day.'

1765 Decisions

Marie did not forget that day in 1759, and neither did Father Michel, but they remembered it differently. Father Michel thought of the occasion less frequently than Marie, but with satisfaction. She had been tamed, she was once again his creature, to be moulded as he willed. She no longer spoke of ungodly reading, really, it was surprising, even a little disappointing, that she had capitulated so quickly. But Marie had not felt remorse on that day, only humiliation. She resolved never again to confide all her thoughts to Father Michel, and especially not her thoughts about the church. She had reasoned to herself that this was justified. After all, the 'sins' recognised by the church, to be told in confession, were very prescribed. One had told lies, or been inattentive at Mass, or lazy in performing one's duties. Reading and thinking could not be sins recognised by the church, so there was no need to tell Father Michel. That did not mean she meant to stop reading, and to cease to think was clearly an impossibility. For what reason had God given us these facilities, except to use them? So she reasoned to herself. Two individuals experienced something together that they could not forget, but they each interpreted it very differently. Such is the isolation of the human soul.

So in subtle ways their relationship changed. Father Michel ascribed Marie's greater reserve to her growing maturity, and welcomed it. Marie felt the loss of intimacy, but at least superficially, she continued to be good friends with Father Michel, and to walk with him in the meadows when she could escape from the drudgery of her service at the Chateau Le Vigin. Father Michel was very fond of her, she knew, and there were so few people to befriend her. Her mother was too busy and thoughtless, her brothers and sisters too young, and the other servants at the chateau, too coarse. She kept herself aloof from them and they thought of her as cold and proud.

She was now nearly seventeen years old, and better read than most girls of her age, even girls of noble birth. Her secret reading both entranced and enraged her. She had read Voltaire's *Candide*, and understood his scathing criticism of the church, implied by his comic character Dr Pangloss, who insists that this is the best possible of all worlds, despite natural disasters such as the Lisbon earthquake in 1755. She had been only seven years old then, when more than thirty thousand people had died. How the people suffered! Some disasters were natural — only God could be blamed. But many were caused by the selfishness of human beings. Her dislike of the nobility, nurtured by the discovery of her birth and inflamed by her reading of *Les Philosophes* had grown with her into young womanhood. This she could discuss with Father Michel, but only as long as she kept silent about her belief that the church itself was implicated in indifference to the suffering of the people.

She thought of these things as she tramped home from the chateau one midsummer evening. The walls of the chateau were covered in honeysuckle, the opening blooms like the mouths of dragons, thought Marie, as she escaped from her detested work. She paused to drink in the voluptuous scent before she started her long walk, passing fields of ancient vines, gnarled like the hands of old women. She passed fields of blood-red hibiscus flowers along the wayside. Blood-red, like the blood they draws from us, thought Marie, resentfully.

'Life is so unfair, Father Michel,' she said to him that evening, during their accustomed walk.

'What in particular is unfair now, my dear Marie?' the priest enquired mildly. He was accustomed to, and tolerated, her interest in matters of social justice. As a nun at the Ursuline Convent in Montauban, the sisters would know how to channel and direct her virtues for the good of the church. The time must come soon, when she would enter, for many of the sisters were far younger than Marie. Father Michel remained resolute in his belief that God would soon grant Marie knowledge of her vocation. Now in his late twenties, he had, if anything, grown in asceticism. His noble forehead seemed higher now the dark hair receded from his temples. His face was finely hewn, as if chiselled of stone, like the figure beside the fountain in the formal garden of the chateau, thought Marie, fondly. In many ways, he remained her idol.

'God's will be done,' the priest murmured abstractedly, consumed with his own thoughts.

'Precisely, Father,' responded Marie. 'How can it be that some should live so extravagantly, in such riches, while others are scraping and scratching just to keep alive? Why, you should see the *food* that is thrown out from the Chateau. Great lumps of meat thrown to the dogs, piles of cabbages in heaps, fruit mouldering and rotting on the vines... it is appalling, when many go hungry.'

'Marie, please do not speak of such things,' said the priest. He was fastidious, and often hungry. Marie continued with her theme, in growing passion.

'But as you know, Father, it is worse for some people in other countries, countries which are governed by France. Why, you told me yourself, when I was quite young, about the slavery of the negroid people in the French colonies. How can it be right that one person claims to own another, claims ownership of the very soul of another? Then, to mistreat these people so badly that their lives are worse than those of animals!'

'Indeed, it must be wrong to ill-treat people and right to show Christian charity to the slaves,' responded Father Michel, giving the matter some thought. 'But remember, Marie, what great good the French people have brought to the colonies. Without the influence of Holy Church, these people would be infidels. What greater good could there be than to bring their souls to Almighty God? What can it matter, how their short earthly lives are lived, if they gain Paradise at the end of this mortal slavery?'

Privately, Marie was more preoccupied with the evils of mortal slavery than the promise of Paradise. Paradise seemed too far away, too nebulous to concern her. But she had learned to keep silent when Father Michel spoke of the church, as indeed he frequently did. He continued,

'You must learn to moderate your thoughts, Marie. Speak more guardedly. You have read a great deal, sometimes of matters which should not concern you. You are merely a girl, but a child no longer. I am, perhaps, too indulgent towards you.'

'I think not, Father.' She laughed, ruefully. 'You sometimes gave me harder penances than the other children. I have not forgotten. But you are right, that I am no longer a child and cannot be treated as such.' She spoke soberly and looked at him searchingly. He returned her gaze, and taking her face into both his hands, asked,

'Marie, do you ever think of your future?'

'No, Father, I do not!' Marie responded gaily. She spoke lightly; her mood, seldom predictable, had quickly changed. 'The present is quite bad enough for me. Especially as most of it is spent crawling on my hands and knees, like an insect!'

She remains a child, thought the priest. *I must be patient.*

Though it was evening, the heat was like a great warm blanket as Marie covered the last half kilometre of her homeward walk, trudging to the end of the lane of the village of Pont d'Herault. She stumbled in deep ridges made by cart-wheels; it had not rained for several weeks. Her feet hurt badly, for it was two years since she had had new boots, and these pinched her unmercifully. At last she pushed open the door of her parents' house. It always stuck, and required more effort than she cared to make after a hard day's work, a long walk home and a slightly unnerving talk with Father Michel. She ran her fingers through her long, fair hair and sank down wearily on the stone floor. It was gloomy inside the cottage. The stew bubbled over the fire. Large black flies hovered over the pot. There was a faint but unmistakable smell of urine mixed with the smell of cooking meat, for there were seven children now. In her weariness Marie had closed her eyes. She opened them, sensing her father's arrival, hearing his heavy tramp through the door. Both her mother and father stood looking at her.

'Well, girl,' began her father. 'I've been waiting for you. Where do you get to in the evenings? Mooning with that young fool of a priest, I've no doubt. More a woman than a man, that one! But it's time you grew away from such foolish talk. It's time we spoke of your marriage.'

'My what, Father?' faltered Marie. Minutes passed, though they felt like hours.

'Don't act the child. Your marriage, I said,' returned Monsieur Cassaigneau.

Despite the weariness that flooded through every limb, Marie rose. Like one of the rabbits in the meadow, when caught in a snare, her eyes widened with fear, but adrenalin rushed through her blood, her noble blood as she believed it to be. She faced him and answered haughtily.

'That can never be, Father. That is impossible. I don't ever mean to marry.'

'You don't *mean to marry,*' mimicked her father. He caught her under the chin. 'You will do what *I mean, my girl!*'

Marie turned to her mother for support, but felt the hopelessness of this. Madame Cassaigneau had grown scraggier now, and if it were possible, even more plaintive. She had cause enough for complaint, with her brood of seven children.

'But Marie, what would you do?' she whined. 'It comes to all women, to be married. What else is there?' Marie searched frantically in her mind. Her mother spoke truly for herself and whole generations of women.

'Why, I can continue working at the chateau, I believe. Perhaps work longer. I could live there if you wished, for I know there is little enough room here. Often and often the housekeeper has asked me to stay, and it would save the journey home. But you have needed my help here with the children, Mother!' Marie pleaded in desperation.

'Your sisters are old enough for all that, now,' interrupted her father. 'Not that I can see much help is needed. The cow does not ask for help in birthing the calf, nor in suckling it.' He shrugged indifferently.

'Marie, it must be better to scrub your own floors, than the floors of the gentry,' wheedled her mother. 'And I swear you will have a grand little floor to call your own.'

'Who... who is it that has offered?' asked Marie, in a scarcely audible voice.

'Why, a man who will know how to master you girl!' answered her father. 'A man of some experience, that's the good thing! But in a respectable station in life, you'll not starve. It is Louis Aubry, the caterer, newly come from Paris.'

Marie felt as if her heart had leaped into her throat. Louis Aubry! The man was neither rich nor well-born, but, far worse, he was old, very old. He was thirty years older than herself. How could she be sacrificed to an old man?

Without another word, Marie ran blindly from the house, choking with tears. As if by instinct she ran up the hill to the church of Our Lady of Sorrows. The priest was kneeling before the statue of the Virgin. With tears streaming down her face, without preamble, she tugged at the kneeling figure of the priest, pulling him, dragging him violently from the object of his devotion, out of the church, into the small walled garden at the back of his cottage. The purple hollyhocks towered majestically at the side of the stone white walls. Blue and white butterflies hovered, drinking from the buddleia. The air was heavy with the scent of velvet-petalled crimson roses. Ever afterwards, Marie hated the smell of a rose garden.

'Father, they would make me marry!' she cried, passionately. He regarded her in silence, showing no emotion, watching her, as the tears coursed down her cheeks and dropped in great splashes onto her worn boots. At length he replied, measuring his words carefully,

'Marie, the proposal was bound to come, eventually. And you abhor the notion?' She nodded, in dumb misery.

'But there is no choice for one such as me. For a poor girl. My father will no longer keep me in the house and he says I may not go to live and work in the chateau. There is no home for me.'

'There is another house you could enter,' he replied. She stared at him uncomprehendingly. The tears dried, leaving long white streaks on her dirty face. She suddenly looked older.

'You mean I could come here? But surely Helene, your housekeeper, would object. Could I really live with you Father?' He turned and paced away from her impatiently. Would she always think like a child? Of course he would love to have her, but it was impossible. Surely she must know that.

'Of course you could not come here, you foolish child. I am a priest, and a young one, at that. The neighbourhood would be shocked, and rightly so. I cannot take a young girl under my roof. But God can.'

'God?'

'Yes. I am sorry your vocation should come to you in this way, so suddenly. I should have hoped it would come, gently, naturally, of your own decision. Not as an alternative to this other thing that you find repugnant. However, better this way than not at all.' He hesitated. The colour rose in his sallow cheeks. The he spoke rapidly. 'You need not think of the dowry that must be paid. I have been putting a little by, each year since you were ten years old, for this very purpose. There will be no difficulty. The Ursuline nuns of Montauban will take care of you.'

'I cannot go to them, Father.'

'What do you mean, you cannot?'

'I have not enough faith. I have no vocation.'

'Yes you have. You *have,* my child. Your vocation will grow. Your faith I have nurtured since you were a child.' The priest was urgent now, insistent on realising his cherished hopes. But the shock of these very ideas calmed Marie. There was some strange bond between them, which she scarcely understood herself, but which bound them together. She could not hurt him, could not disappoint his ideas for her. But still she could not do as he asked. She searched rapidly in her mind for words to explain to him. Never, never would she tell him of the failure of her first Holy Communion... and all subsequent communions. More lately, there had been her silent criticism of the church; this she had learned to keep secret from him. She must prevaricate, to save him pain.

'You know me, Father. You know what a vain creature I am. I... I could not see myself in the habit of the nuns.' He said nothing, so she continued, 'I want to wear lace, and let the wind blow through my hair, not shave it off and hide my bald head, like the nuns. I want pretty things.'

His silence unnerved her. She grew more flippant, 'I want

to put flowers in my hair... and to be admired.'

'Be silent!' he thundered. 'For reasons such as these, you will not enter God's house?'

'These are my reasons, Father.' She knew it was necessary to be determined, to convince him. She loved him and hated to disappoint him so cruelly. But even more, she could not lie to herself, or to God, if God existed. So she lifted her chin pugnaciously.

'I shall not change my mind, Father Michel.'

He looked at her and knew this was true. She had the same look about her as she had when she was a small child, cajoling him into teaching her to read. A steel thread of determination lay within her, to go her own way. The blood of Lefranc De Pompignan, who rode through Languedoc, careless of others, conscious only of his own will, was her blood. A wave of bitter disappointment came over him. He was going to lose her.

'You disappoint me greatly, Marie. I doubt you realise how much. When you reject this, you reject me, for it is the work I have given my life to. Perhaps, even, you reject God.' This was unfair, and Marie knew it. To say God's will was his will, was to seek to close a disagreement without the use of human reason. Her resolve strengthened.

'I cannot help it, father. I cannot help the way I feel. And I have *my life, also!*'

'And you choose to spend it in this way?'

'I've told you, I have no choice... for the present. The man chosen for me is repugnant to me. He is old. Perhaps that may mean I shall live after he is dead. Then perhaps, I may do as I choose.' Her calculating prognosis for her future should have shocked him, but he was too consumed by what was, for him, a bitter rejection of his cherished plan.

'I can think of nothing but my sadness. When you reject this chance, you reject me. It is as if you have taken the Holy Gospels and told me they are worthless. Torn them up and used them with kindling to light a fire!'

Marie shrugged. This was ridiculous.

'That's just nonsense, Father. My feelings cannot affect your religion. Anyway, I will marry,' she added, with a touch of spite, 'of course, you will have to conduct the ceremony of marriage.'

'I cannot.' He was appalled. 'I cannot give you to another man, Marie!'

'You can, and you will. I have to do this thing I hate. It is you who have no choice, now. You are the only priest of Pont d'Herault. I am of your parish. You will have to marry me to this man.'

At last the priest asked, 'Who is the man?'

'You know him well. It is Louis Aubry, the caterer. He is old and ugly.' She thought of his wrinkled skin and slack mouth and added, bitterly, 'I dare say his tongue is already hanging out for me.' Then crudely, maliciously, determined in her anger to shock the priest, she added 'And though he is old I expect he has still a strong grip to squeeze my breasts, do you not think so, Father?'

He turned from her in disgust and re-entered the church. He went again to the plaster doll, the Virgin, to find solace in prayer to her. But comfort did not come to him easily that night. The thoughts of Marie's marriage to Louis Aubry made him feel sick, and in fact he fell ill with a fever and was spared the agony of performing her marriage ceremony. Marie was married at the church of Saint-Jean de Villeneuve in Montauban on October 24th, 1765.

Marie went through the nuptial mass like an automaton. She made her responses in a hard, detached voice and deliberately let her thoughts wander. The fat stone cherubs decorating the font were like the babies she would soon have, she supposed. She shuddered; better not think of that. She looked instead at the greasy yellow candles on the altar. The coils of wax encrusting the candlesticks looked like the pictures of coral she had seen in one of the books in the library of the Chateau Le Vigin. She would never see real coral now, or the sea, or the far-off hot countries where black people lived and toiled in slavery. She would spend her days in domestic drudgery and her nights on her back, with the ageing body of Louis Aubry crushing her.

'I will,' she repeated, tonelessly.

Madame Cassaigneau sniffed audibly. Marie's stepfather, standing beside her, smiled complacently, thinking with satisfaction that he would at last rid himself of the responsibility of this irritating bastard girl. The priest who officiated noted that the bride was scarcely more than a child. She was wearing a coarse, white calico gown to denote her virginity, such as she had worn for her first Holy Communion. The gown was quite plain. She had not bothered with the struggle to obtain lace for this occasion. There were no flowers in her hair. When the time came for the hosts to be distributed the priest noted the little pink tongue Marie held out trustingly. He pitied her and tried not to look at the slack mouth of the man kneeling beside her. The great slug of a tongue, between black teeth, was flattened before the priest, like a deliberate insult. An odour of garlic emitted from it. The black stubbly hairs on the top lip were already bedewed with sweat, despite the cool of the nave of the church.

The rest of the day passed in a daze for Marie. That night she lay in the lumpy bed of the caterer's house and screwed her eyes tight shut as her husband pulled together the curtains and doused the light. Never had she found her prayers so efficacious. She managed to say the *Hail Mary* three times before the lovemaking was finished and Louis rolled off her, grunting. Then he lay in the middle of the bed, his legs spread-eagled, his mouth a malodorous, open cavern. She inched herself to the edge of the bed and held on tightly. It was dawn before she slept.

1766 Childbirth

Louis Aubry sat in the kitchen, eating his *daube d'agneau* in solitary gloom; he frowned as he dipped his hunk of bread into the sauce. There was nothing wrong with the stew, which had been prepared by his mother-in-law, but he was disturbed by the noise from the chamber above the stairs. *Really, what a fuss and bother was made by women at the time of childbirth!* he thought. It was after all, a natural process, although sadly, one that disturbed a man's domestic comfort. Not that he had experienced much comfort from his young wife. She was comely enough, but remote, cold, and sometimes, he fancied, disdainful in the way she looked at him. Worse, she made no effort to disguise her distaste for her marital duties. Surprising really, that one brought up with the beasts of the field should be so squeamish. He had tried to rouse some warmth in her; he was, after all, thirty years older than her, with plenty of experience in the beds of women. It would never have occurred to him that his ageing body was itself the cause of her disgust, but he could not disguise from himself that this was a child conceived without love.

Marie's mother was upstairs in the airless bedchamber. The bed had been pulled out into the centre of the room and there were old rags tied to the bedposts for when the time came for bearing down. Marie had not asked what the rags were for. She looked very small lying in the bed, apart from the great mound of her stomach.

'You might be better walking around, *ma chere*,' said her mother. 'You've a long way to go yet.' Marie shook her head. A wave of pain passed over her and she closed her eyes.

'Was it bad?' asked her mother.

Marie nodded. 'Does it get worse, *Maman?*'

'A little,' her mother lied. She knew the child would not be born for some hours yet. Marie was merely on the threshold of pain. The day wore on, the sun's rays pierced relentlessly into the room, increasing the suffering of the labouring girl. For a time, between pains, she dozed and dreamed of the waves of the sea, which she had never seen. Each wave gathered and rolled towards the shore, then broke in bursts of creamy foam. Then she awoke and found that the waves were real, pain more intense than she could ever have imagined. There were moments of bliss, the cessation of pain, then the next wave gathered, the muscle swelled, rippled and writhed, gathering itself for the next crash, intent on expelling the baby from the womb.

'It might be better to cry out?' asked Madame Cassaigneau, gently. She had seen many babies born, had borne many herself, but had never witnessed such stoic indifference. Marie's forehead was creased, but no murmur came from her. Her concentration was centred in the middle of her body. She was apart from the world, yet vaguely aware of sensations around her, her husband's pacing downstairs, the bluebottle buzzing irritatingly at the window, the shadows of evening lengthening, yet bringing no cooling air to the stifling room, the light of the candle showing up threadbare patches in the curtains. Time ceased for her.

At around ten o'clock, the head crowned. Still Marie showed no excitement but dutifully hoisted herself up in the bed and, taking hold of the rags above her head, began the business of pushing the baby out into the world. Her forehead was creased into a ferocious frown, her teeth clamped together and she snarled in her efforts. Madame Cassaigneau peered beneath the sheets and saw the crown of the baby's head, encrusted and covered in a whorl of wet, black hair. The protruding head emerged and the mother reached down to the lips of her daughter's body, stretched to breaking point. With her finger, she reached around the child's neck, to free the mucus from the mouth. With one more instinctive effort, Marie expelled the child from her womb. It lay, face downwards on the lumpy mattress, between its mother's legs. Madame Cassaigneau turned the child onto its back and Marie looked down. It was a boy. He was like a fat, pink, slime encrusted slug, she thought. Her mother picked him up and he screamed lustily, waving his little arms about like the tendrils of a sea anemone.

'A fine boy, Marie. Look at him,' said her mother. She placed the baby in her daughter's arms; he rooted and fastened onto her breast like a limpet, sucking vigorously.

'Well there, he has the right idea already!' exclaimed her mother. Marie looked down at the baby in her arms, but said nothing. She allowed him to suck for a few more moments and then, using her little finger, unplugged the small mouth from her breast and handed him to her mother. Silently, she motioned her to lay him in the makeshift cradle, fashioned from a split wine barrel. Turning from the cradle, she slept.

For fourteen days after the birth it was the custom for the

mother to lie in bed, her stomach bound tightly with rags, festering in the smell of her own blood. She was only allowed to wash the top part of her body; the baby was brought to her for feeding. But by the fourth day Marie was delirious, fever had set in. She raved of the seashore, of the waves crashing on the sea at Les Landes, crashing all over the world, swallowing up the slave people of Guyana. They were dying and drowning in far-off oceans.

'See, they are falling into the waves, none can save them... I wanted to save them... I wanted to try...' she cried out in her delirium.

'Hush my love, you do not know what you say... try to feed the child,' implored her mother. But Marie shook her head, tossing her straggling fair locks away from her burning head and throwing off the bedclothes wildly. She had no interest in the child, she could not feed him; she was near to suffocation as the fever raged and engulfed her, in the stifling, airless room.

'The waves are crashing onto the shore... I dreamed of seeing them... let me see them once before I die...' Marie muttered. 'Open the window that I may feel the sea breeze and be free as the sea-birds. The birds fly as high as Heaven... I have dreamed I was a bird... I have dreamed I was free.'

'My child, you are in a fever. I cannot let in the air.'

'Let me feel the air once more before I die,' murmured Marie.

'I cannot. Be still my child,' begged Madame Cassaigneau.

'Mother... do you think people can ever be free...?.can they be free like the seagulls, do you think?' Marie muttered, as she lapsed into a fitful sleep.

Madame Cassaigneau checked that the casement was firmly fastened. Should her daughter rise from her bed, she must not be able to let in the treacherous air. It was unlikely she would have the strength to do so. She feared Marie would die from the childbirth fever, after all, so many women did so. She lifted the child from his cradle, where he whimpered fretfully. The lusty cries with which he had first greeted the world were becoming more feeble. Downstairs, Louis Aubry sat silently eating the bread and cheese she had hastily prepared for him. He was sulking, that he was expected to endure these makeshift meals. He turned his head away as his mother-in-law silently took the child outside and walked with him down to the village where her husband's cows were tethered. Something must be done, to sustain this infant.

Meanwhile Father Michel rose from his knees, after long prayer. He genuflected deeply to the Virgin and, closing the church door firmly behind him, walked purposefully towards the village. It was a heavy, thundery day; the sky looked curdled and the road glared as he looked down at it, deep in thought. Clouds of dust swirled over his shoes as he strode purposefully forward. He knew what he must do. A child was born. It behoved him, the parish priest, to enquire of its welfare and the well-being of the child's mother. Since the marriage of Marie and Louis Aubry, he had avoided all intercourse with them except during his formal duties at Mass, but of course he knew what he must do at this time. He must ensure the child's parents brought it to baptism.

Louis Aubry's mournful, self-pitying reflections were disturbed by a sharp rap at the door. Obtaining no response, the priest pushed his shoulder to the door and entered, uninvited. A scene of shocking disarray met his eyes. Boots and bedclothes lay scattered on the floor. Half-eaten food, dirty plates and knives lay strewn at the large wooden table. There sat Louis Aubry, gloomily eating bread and cheese.

'Good afternoon sir,' said Father Michel. 'I have come to enquire after your wife and child, and to know when you mean to bring the child for baptism. Your wife, also, must be churched, since she has given birth.'

'They tell me you are more likely to be called upon to give her the last rites,' replied Aubry, with asperity. 'Although I cannot think that she is so ill. After all, it is the duty of women to bring children into the world.'

Father Michel, was silent, aghast. Childbirth was indeed a procedure far removed from his knowledge. Could it really be the case that Marie might die? The idea was impossible, too horrible to contemplate.

'Is she really so ill? May I see her... and... and the child?'

'Hardly so. She lies abed, raving in her fever. And the grandmother has taken the child to her house, while I am left here, unattended, and expected to eat left-over scraps not fit for the pigs!' he concluded, in tones of great disgust.

'I am sorry for you sir,' said Father Michel, untruthfully. He looked at the old man more closely and saw that indeed, he looked fretful and unwell. But he could not concern himself with the husband.

'Perhaps I had better enquire of Madame Cassaigneau,' he said, turning to the door. He left the house abruptly and returned to the village.

At length he reached the police house. Outside, in the

yard, an extraordinary sight met his eyes. Marie's mother, squatting on a milking stool, held out the infant to the teats of a tethered cow. The infant latched greedily onto the cow's teats and sucked greedily. Its tiny tentacles of hands were clutching and pummelling at the cow's udders. Father Michel was repelled at the sight. It was so animal, so earthy. Yet the grandmother held out the child with infinite patience, a look of joy on her face as if the child was an oblation to the gods. So absorbed were the grandmother and child in their task that they did not notice the arrival of the priest.

'What are you doing, Madame Cassaigneau?' called the priest, at last.

'Why, Father, it is as clear as daylight, what I am doing. I am feeding my grandson. Come closer, see for yourself how well he sucks.' The priest did not move.

'You cannot do so... it... is... obscene!'

'I cannot do else, since his mother lies close to death in childbed fever!' she retorted sharply. 'What would you have me do? Let the child starve?' So saying, she carefully detached the baby from the cow's teat, and, with infinite gentleness, placed him upon her shoulder. 'Come inside, Father. Take a glass of wine, since you've troubled to walk so far in the heat,' she added, suddenly hospitable.

Inside the house, Madame Cassaigneau laid the child down gently on a rug on the floor and bustled about with the carafe of wine. Father Michel asked her, in great fear,

'Marie? Is she so very ill?'

The mother shrugged. She was far from indifferent to the fate of her daughter, but life had taught her to face grim realities, at least, where childbirth was concerned.

'Who can say? She is young and strong, she may yet recover. It is the chance women take, sir, all women.' She smiled sardonically. 'Surely you would say, Father, it is in the hands of God?'

Father Michel made no answer. He turned from her and looked at the child. Inside the foetid interior of the cottage, detached from the cow's teat, he was able to see him more clearly. In the last week he had thought a great deal about this unfortunate infant, almost as much as he had thought about its mother. He had deliberated long about its soul, its welfare, its unhappy inheritance. But as a celibate, he had thought about the child as an abstraction, a moral principle. Now he was confronted with the living reality, lying on a dirty rug. It was a living, wriggling, bundle of humanity. It was a thing of flesh and bones and blood which would one day stand on its feet and walk independently. It would think private thoughts and other thoughts it would share in talk with people, and would agree or disagree when other people talked with it. It was a life, and its life was a glorious fact given to the world by this man and woman, by God's grace. It was not a moral principle any longer. It was a child. A boy, he noted. *He* was a child.

Father Michel stooped and picked up the child. Tentatively, very carefully, he lifted him and cradled him in his arms.

'He is a fine child, Madame,' he said.

'Indeed, Father. I think he has a look of his grandfather.' She smiled meaningfully. 'His *real grandfather,* that is.' Father Michel ignored this. The child absorbed his attention.

'He is a fine boy,' he repeated. 'But he is very dirty. We must wash him.'

'Pah! He does very well as he is,' replied the grandmother. 'Feeding, yes, that is important. But washing? Why, that is women's work and to say the truth, Father, between his poor sick mother and his grumbling father, not to mention my own family, I have enough to do!'

'Nevertheless, I shall wash him,' said the priest, decisively. He laid the child gently back on the rug and turned to the stove. Amongst the debris on the table he saw an earthenware bowl. He swilled it out with water from the copper pot on the stove and wiped it carefully with the end of his cassock. He poured in hot water, then cold, and tested the temperature carefully with his long, tapering fingers. Then, taking the child in his arms again, he unwrapped the layers of grime encrusted bandages that swathed the small limbs, until finally he held in his arms, a living, kicking image of bronze.

'How brown he is!' he exclaimed. 'As brown as a nut. Who would have thought so? His mother is so fair.'

'I told you, Father, he is very like his maternal grandfather. Thanks be to God, for his father is not comely!'

Gently, the priest washed the child, while his grandmother squatted on the stool, watching the priest as he attended to the child. The baby splashed and kicked, joyfully agitated by the freedom of his limbs. Soon he was clean. Father Michel looked about the room for a towel, but there seemed to be none, so he continued to hold the baby in his lap and dabbed at him with the end of his cassock. The baby lay in his lap, a kicking bronze cherub, a writhing, seething bundle of life. Madame Cassaigneau looked at the priest curiously;

'Well, Father I must thank you. You are fond of my daughter, are you not? You always gave her great attention, when she was a child, growing up.'

'Yes,' he replied briefly. 'I wished for a different life for her.'

She laughed. 'Ah, Father, Marie will go her own way. Should she live, she will go her own way again. She is her father's child, not yours!'

Marie did live. Several weeks later she walked out into the meadows beyond the church, with Father Michel. It was September; the days were cooler now and the clouds scudded across the sky. The leaves had turned to orange and gold. They fluttered down on the breeze, down to the brown earth, newly turned since the cutting of the hay. Great cylinders of golden hay lay under the trees at the edge of the meadow, awaiting the cart drawn by oxen, which would collect them. A light drizzle was falling.

'Well, Marie,' said Father Michel cheerfully, 'you have recovered and have a fine son. I must wish you joy of him.'

'Yes,' she replied, flatly. 'I am responsible for his life. That I know. I shall do what I can for him.'

'You must next consider your duties. There is his baptism to arrange, and the churching ceremony must take place for you.' Marie did not reply immediately. Then she said, very carefully,

'The baptism I have considered. I shall give him a name. It will be Pierre. He will be Pierre Aubry, for he cannot take his true name, his grandfather's name. He must take the name of his low-born father.'

Father Michel ignored much of what she was saying. He was well aware of Marie's rancour, her child-like obsession with the rejection of her natural father. She was still fragile, since childbirth. Now was not the time to argue with her. He replied to her choice of Christian name, enthusiastically,

'Well chosen!' The name of our blessed St Peter, the first of all popes!'

'I had not thought of that,' said Marie. 'I like the name, that is all. As for the other thing, that is called the Purification, I will not have it. I have suffered much. I almost died.' She continued, with more passion, 'Do you know, Father, that giving birth to a child is like going down to the gates of Hell? You do not know and you will never know. No man could endure what is suffered by women. What we do in the bedchamber is done for the pleasure of men, yet it is women who bear the consequences. Why, on this account am I to be considered impure?'

'It is the custom,' he replied stiffly. 'The ceremony is required by Holy Church, to purify women after childbirth.'

'Such an answer cannot satisfy me' she said. 'I repeat, I will not have it. I shall tell you something else. Last night, I refused my husband's demands. That also, you will tell me, is a sin. I must submit to him that I may once more become *enceinte,* and give birth to another child. Then once more I shall be in a state of sin.' Her voice rose on a note of hysteria. She laughed aloud. 'It seems to me there is altogether too much talk of sin. But never for men!'

He looked at her pityingly, yet there was a note of triumph in his voice as he replied,

'It is so, I agree. But it is the life you chose!'

'I told you before, Father, I had *no choice!*' she cried, stamping her foot in her frustration, that he would not or could not understand. 'I cannot be like the nuns in the convent, or...

or like *her!*' She pointed wildly, angrily, in the direction of the church. He knew she meant the statue.

'Marie, what is your meaning?' he asked. Inwardly, he was enraged by her blasphemy, but deemed it best to approach her gently, while this mood lasted.

'I hardly know, Father. I... I find it difficult to love my child. He reminds me too much of his father, and all that I have suffered.' She paused and added, with more resolution, 'But, as I have said, I shall do my best for him.'

'Well Marie, he is a fine child, your son. And that is something I shall never have.' She looked into his face and saw the sadness there. Infuriating as he was, she pitied and loved him.

1770 Flight to Paris

Marie sat in the meadow above her mother's house, deep in thought. It was a beautiful day in early spring; there was a gentle breeze and blossoms were emerging on the apple trees. The air and the grass smelled of new growth. In her lap she cradled the dead body of a young rabbit. She had found it, bloodied, with its neck snapped in a trap, at the edge of the meadow. *Poor young rabbit*, she thought. Yet perhaps it was better to have a short life, a life of freedom before the quick, sudden ending in the trap. She had thought a great deal lately, about freedom. She remembered that, when her son was about to be born, and afterwards in the delirium of her fever, she had imagined she was a seagull, flying as high as the clouds. The waves of pain had become the waves of the endless sea, crashing on the shore. She remembered those feelings well. There was a kind of pleasure, remembering the oblivion of those times. It was the kind of feeling she had when she tried to stay asleep, to prevent waking to harsh reality.

For the last three years, she had felt as if the trap was creeping closer, waiting to ensnare her. There had been some hope after the death of her husband, for Louis Aubry had died less than a year after the birth of his son. He was worn out, she believed, by the foolish lusts of an ageing body, by his stupidity and arrogance in taking a young wife. Marie had felt no grief, and refused to pretend to any such feelings. In the same way, she felt only relief when her stepfather, Dominique-Raymond Cassaigneau, followed him to the grave in less than twelve months. She had not loved these men in their lifetimes and it was dishonest to pretend to do so now they were dead. She agreed to wear black, but that was all. She had moved back to her mother's house and to her servant's work in the Chateau Le Vigin. All the same, life could not continue as it was. Her mother was left poor and, never a great one for coping with the demands of a large, boisterous family, found it increasingly difficult to manage. Her grandson, Pierre, was a demanding and difficult child. Much as she loved him, Madame Cassaigneau wanted to remove him and Marie from her household. Ever an optimist, she felt that that the best solution was for her eldest daughter to marry again, if possible to marry well. Then perhaps her new son-in-law might be induced to help his wife's family. So reasoned Madame Cassaigneau; she had been romantic since her girlhood and was unlikely to listen to the voice of reason now she was growing old.

Marie had vowed to herself that she would never marry again. She believed she had been sacrificed, for no good reason, to a man who was old and repugnant to her. Never again would she allow such a thing to happen. The institution of marriage itself she saw as a bondage to women. But how could she explain this to those around her, who had thought and read so little, indeed who had read nothing at all? How could she explain the ideas she had been nurturing since her childhood, since the priest had first taught her to read. Most women saw marriage as their inevitable lot, that, or the cloister.

Father Michel was himself another snare in the trap. If she

loved any man, she loved him. But she had long ago learned to keep her doubts about religion to herself, mostly out of consideration for his sensibilities. Yet sometimes it was impossible to do so. For he still cherished beliefs about what he saw as the future for Marie Gouze, to enter the Ursuline Convent. A week ago they had spoken of it again.

'Father, I tell you again that I could never do so,' Marie had said, emphatically. She sought to make light of the matter, to avoid telling him of her true reasons. 'The vows the nuns take, they would be impossible for me. Poverty? Well that would be easy, I confess. The sisters do not want for anything. True, they do not live in luxury, but they have no notion of the fear felt by so many, of poverty and starvation. Chastity?' She laughed. 'Well, that again would not be difficult. After the experiences I have had in marriage, a life of chastity would seem like rest and peace. But, Father, you know me, how headstrong I am. Never, never, could I consent to being *obedient!*'

He had avoided answering her objections directly, but remarked, somewhat obscurely,

'You know, Marie, it is possible that some of the sisters do not feel what I have called a vocation. Perhaps they enter the convent because it is a life which is preferable for them. Perhaps, like you, they recoil from marriage. You have said you will not marry again. Would it not be better to become a nun?'

She had been startled by what she saw as his advocacy of personal dishonesty.

'Never! How could such a thing be better, since it would be a lie?'

'Who would know?' he replied, quietly.

'*I would know*,' she replied, vehemently. She continued more quietly, as if speaking to herself... ' and God would know.'

She thought about this conversation now. What had she meant? She was not sure. She was not really sure she believed in God. Even if she did, she could not *love God.* For Marie, the idea was empty, meaningless. For Father Michel had told her himself, God is omnipotent, eternal, present in all times and places. He is not a man, and for that reason alone, is too remote, too obscure, too unimaginable for *love!* For Father Michel it was easy. He said that he had always loved God. She envied him; it must be comforting to feel the presence of God. Perhaps one was born that way, born to believe. But if belief did not come, well, it simply did not. Perhaps she was too stupid, but yet she thought not, for she was very good at imagining other things, the life she might have if she could live in Paris in a beautiful apartment, to visit the *salons philosophiques,* to meet lively, educated and intelligent people. These things should all have been her birth right, if her real father, the marquis, had recognised her as his daughter, Always, her troubles reverted to him and his rejection of her.

She thought more about the love of God. Although she found this so hard to conceptualise, she felt she could have loved Jesus, if she had known him in the flesh. Perhaps she could imagine loving Jesus because she thought of him as the image of Father Michel, the same tall stature and melting brown eyes. The same way of speaking, gently, but with authority. She had ventured to say, when they last met,

'Father, I know you do not like me to find fault with the

church. But I do think it is such a pity that it has decreed that priests should not marry. Why, have you not thought, it would be an answer to my problem. I could marry you! What do you think of that idea?' She had laughed flirtatiously, to detract from the serious nature of her criticism.

'That could not be, Marie. In a way I see it is a pity, yes, for I also love you. But those who follow in the footsteps of Christ must be celibate, as he was.'

'How do we know?' responded Marie. 'He was a Jew, was he not? It is most unusual for Jewish men to remain celibate, even today, is it not? And Jesus did have women friends, Martha, and Mary Magdalene. How do we know that he was celibate? Perhaps it is simply not the sort of thing people wrote about, when they wrote the Gospels. After all, the affairs of women are not generally considered to be of any importance, certainly not worth writing about!' she had concluded, on a note of bitterness. Not for the first time, Father Michel wondered if he had done his dear Marie a great disservice in teaching her to be literate. She had continued her reading far beyond what was necessary or desirable, to content her for the life she must lead. And what was that life to be, since she refused to enter the convent?

These thoughts preoccupied Marie as she sat in the meadow, nursing the dead body of the rabbit. She could not continue as she was. There was another proposition which she must consider carefully. Several weeks ago, she had been caught in the library of the Chateau Le Vigin, by the young Comte de Blois, a visitor to the chateau. It was a wonder that this had never happened before, for Marie was still an avid reader and frequently slipped in to borrow a book. She had been caught replacing Rousseau's *Emile* on the library shelves. The young comte was a tall, elegant young man with curly brown locks flowing to his shoulders. He had been amused when he saw what she was reading;

'Unusual tastes for a serving girl!' he had said. 'I wonder what you think of it?'

'Very highly sir,' she had stammered. I... I think he writes well, when he writes of the child, Emile, being allowed to grow in freedom, to pursue his own interests. He writes, *"Emile knows little, but what he knows is his own"*. The young man had smiled; she intrigued him.

'And what do you know, *mademoiselle?*'

'Also very little, sir. But I learn what I can, for I take great joy in reading.'

'Strange, for a girl, especially one of your station in life!'

'It is not the station I was born to, sir!' she had retorted. 'Nor one that I would occupy, if I could choose.'

Since then they had spoken on several occasions, for the young comte was growing daily more interested in Marie. He was a young man of fortune, accustomed, as he told Marie, to having his own way. He determined to make the young girl his mistress. He was bored; it would be amusing to take this girl. She had a little experience, for she told him of her short marriage. She had not responded with ardour when he kissed her, but she had not drawn back either. She was very different from the general run of Parisian courtesans. He needed a change, some refreshment to add a little piquancy to his languid life. He proposed to take her to Paris, in his protection. He was waiting for her answer.

Marie thought of this now. From every sensible

perspective, it was the best possible chance she had to escape. She must try to explain this to Father Michel. She wanted so much for him to understand why she had to do this, even though she knew it was impossible for him to approve of her intentions. She wanted him to *accept her choice*. She could not leave for Paris without telling him, for in ways she could scarcely explain, she felt that she belonged to him. Three days later they met. The clouds were like great pillows in a translucent aquamarine sky as they walked together. The grass was growing high and the skirts of Father Michel's cassock made a swishing sound as they walked through it. Dusk was falling and rooks were cawing from the tops of the poplar trees, newly in leaf.

'Father, I must speak to you,' she began, firmly. 'Please listen to me. I have been asked by the young Comte de Blois to accompany him to Paris. He... he admires me. He will be kind, I think, and he offers to take my son as well. I do not love Henri de Blois, of course, nor does he love me. But it is a chance, is it not? I know he will soon tire of me. But in the meantime, I shall meet interesting, cultured people. It is a chance to improve myself, to find others who have read what I have read, to talk with them and to learn more of the thoughts of the great writers of our day. The comte does not speak of marriage, of course, and I am glad of that, for as I have told you, never again will I marry. But neither can I enter the convent, for reasons I have also explained. It would be dishonest. That, to me, is the greatest sin.'

Father Michel looked into her face. Then he turned and walked away. She heard his voice saying,

'And you call this honest? You call it a *chance!* To become a whore!'

'*Courtesan,* is a more polite name, I believe. Yes, I think for one such as I am, with no acknowledged birth right, it is the only chance. I would prefer that it was not so. But God has not made a perfect world, not for women, at least.'

'And you will feel no shame?' he asked, still with his back turned to her.

'No, I think not.' She continued flippantly, *"Ca lui fait tant de plaisir, et moi si peu de peine."* This was spoken, I believe, by the actress, Jeanne Gaussain. Men want it, and it is so little trouble for me.' She paused for a moment and then continued, as if speaking to herself, 'I do not think I could act, I have no talent for pretence. But I have a great liking for the theatre. Perhaps I shall write a play.'

He turned at last and she saw, to her astonishment, that he was silently weeping. Great tears were flowing down his cheeks. She had expected his anger, his moral outrage and his pious disapproval But she had not expected this.

'Why, Father Michel, do not weep for me. I shall do very well. I shall confess my sins from time to time, I suppose. Do not concern yourself with me, I pray you.'

'I weep for myself, Marie' he replied, in strangled tones. 'I weep because I shall lose you. You say it is what men want. I, too, want you.'

She walked towards him and laid her hands on his shoulders, seeking to comfort him. 'Why, Father you will not lose me. I shall return, from time to time, to see my mother and to see you.' But inwardly she was thinking, *so after all, he is the same. A thousand years of possessiveness, caught in the yoke of manhood. He is a man, after all.* Never had she loved him more than when she told him she was leaving.

1770 Early Months in Paris

The young Comte de Blois sprawled with one well-breeched leg elegantly across the other on the chaise longue at the back of the stage box of the Paris Opera, regarding with satisfaction the profile of his mistress. In particular, he was admiring the diamond baubles hanging from her little ear; they gleamed in the light of the chandelier as she leaned forward, eagerly intent upon the action on the stage beneath. It was pleasant to be able to adorn so beautiful a creature, without feeling the cost. God! How beautiful she looked. One could still detect in this young girl, the virgin who by the merest chance had become a courtesan. He supposed he was fortunate to have discovered her while she was so young, before she became — as she inevitably would — raddled and cynical, grasping, like the general run of Parisian courtesans. Involuntarily, he stretched forward and caressed the curls at her neck; she flinched, turned her head a little and, with a frightened little smile and a shake of her head, indicated that she would prefer to watch the play. Henri de Blois scowled and sat back; this was not the first time she had rebuffed him. Unfortunately his little whore from Languedoc seemed not to know how a mistress should behave. For what were the chaise longues so conveniently placed in the opera boxes, if not for the indulgence of a little amorous dalliance, when — as was the case now — the play grew tedious? Everyone knew that Parisians did not come to the theatre to see the performance, but to meet and be met and to pursue the fascinating arts of love and intrigue. Marie evidently had not learned this yet. She was socially inept and unskilled in the arts of pleasing; she was gauche, and there were times, when he introduced her to his friends, when he felt ashamed of his raw little country girl, for all her beauty. He had tried to school her, but, in truth, after three months, his patience was running out. There were limits to the efforts one should have to make with an expensive little item like a mistress.

He had not expected to have to school her in the bedchamber. But she was damnably cold; is was like clasping a creature of porcelain to your breast. Really, she seemed not to know the first rules of the career she had embarked upon, of her own free will, he assured himself, for it had taken very little to persuade her to leave the country and establish herself in Paris under his protection. Well, she would soon learn that a lover's protection was short-lived if his mistress behaved like a shrinking virgin in the bedchamber, and she a wife and mother before he had ever set eyes on her! No, he assured himself, there had been no seduction in the case. He was twenty-two years of age and this was his fourth mistress, so he knew the rules of the game. Never give a courtesan anything with which to reproach you. Give to her generously as long as she pleases your fancy, but be sure to exact your dues. Pay her handsomely, and pay her off when you have tired of her. In the case of Marie Gouze, it had only taken three months for their little liaison to run its inevitable course. He had hoped for something better, but why repine? There were plenty of others, sensuous, willing and properly schooled, who knew what a lover required.

In truth, Marie was not particularly engrossed in the play, although it was her studied intention to make Henri think she was, in order to ward off, just for a while, his incessant attentions. She was well aware that in doing so she was making a dangerous mistake. His interest in her was fading already, she knew, and she was beginning to realise, with increasing panic, that without him she would be utterly destitute. He had been generous with jewels and clothes, and *livres* for her to spend and adorn herself, but she had been reckless with his money and had saved nothing. More foolishly, she had allowed herself to show him her repugnance in the bedchamber. Yet she could not help herself. Almost from the time of her arrival in Paris it had become clear to her that the bed of the young comte was not markedly different from the bed of her old husband. Henri smelled a little fresher, but was almost equally repellent to her. In fact, his demands were even more urgent and his attitude more demanding, since, she thought bitterly, he was young and paid for that which he demanded. She liked his presents and she liked to be clothed in diamonds and lace. She did not mind talking with him either, though she found his conversation a little frivolous and tedious. If only, she thought, they would leave you *alone!* Instead, they pressed and mauled you, exactly as if you were a carcase on the butcher's slab. It was like a grotesque kind of animal dissection, the way they wanted to examine and expose you. It reminded her of the fact that the man who had passed to the world as her father, Pierre Gouze, had been a butcher. In her mind, he and Louis Aubry were intrinsically mixed.

Perhaps, she mused, that was why she had never wanted

to marry anyone. She could clearly remember certain dreadful scenes between her so-called father and her mother, scenes she had witnessed when she was a small child. They had left a secret wound in her mind. And then, her mother had seemed as a result of these scenes, to be forever enduring the monstrosity that was childbirth, just as she herself had done. In her mind, memories of the abattoir and the marriage bed were inextricably linked. Then there was the horror of childbirth. Somehow, with some advice from those she would meet, she must find the means of avoiding the difficulty of being constantly *enceinte*. Pierre was established with her in Paris, and for that she was grateful to Henri de Blois. She was beginning to love her child, a little. But she wanted no more. And whatever became of her liaison with Henri, she could never return to her former life. Somehow, she must establish herself in Paris.

Her mind wandered to her girlhood. Perhaps it would have been different with that other man, with his dark aquiline face and his saintly eyes. She concentrated on bringing his image into her mind, trying to imagine Father Michel in the act of love. It was impossible. Just because of his fastidious habits and his austerity and distant refinement, it was impossible. Probably that was why she loved him, because it was impossible to think of him behaving as other men. And yet, at their last meeting, he had intimated that he *was* as other men. Somehow the thought thrilled her; he should be her lover in a world of fantasy. She would love him in a mixture of utter fantasy and total unreality, and their love would never get bogged down with anything as silly as being real. It should be her secret amulet, her talisman. There were other secrets, after all. She was glad she had never told him of her true reasons for refusing the life of the cloister. He would never understand her failure to believe in God. She could have pretended, of course, and almost, he had suggested she should. It was impossible to be sure of his meaning. She had tried pretending to truly believe and for a while she had almost convinced herself. She could have convinced him, she could have taken in everyone, she thought, Father Michel, her mother, even some hard-faced mother superior. Everyone except herself and God. And there would not have been much point in that. So it would always be her secret, even from her secret lover. It was between her and God.

A firm grasp on her naked arm interrupted her thoughts and returned her abruptly to the present reality. The comte was indicating, imperiously as always, that he wished to leave the theatre. Meekly, she gathered her wrap and allowed his arm to encircle her waist as he escorted her from the theatre to their waiting carriage. He did not speak until they were ensconced in the privacy of the carriage; then he instructed her briefly;

'Marie, tonight a few of my intimate friends will gather at my house for supper. They will be persons of fashion and wit, to whom I shall introduce you. I beg you will conduct yourself with charm and gaiety, as befits my mistress and the hostess of my party.'

Almost, she dreaded these fashionable gatherings as much as she dreaded the more intimate duties of her new life. She wanted to meet cultivated and well-informed people, but these friends were more likely to indulge in bawdy raillery, and she felt inadequate in taking her part in the extravagant orgies which the comte found so entertaining. But, with belated caution, and perhaps because she had been thinking about pretence in quite a different situation, she replied, dutifully, 'I shall try to please, my Lord.'

'You had better succeed, my dear.' Then he added, meaningfully, 'You had better succeed also, when we retire to the bedchamber, afterwards. That is, if you wish to remain the mistress of the Comte de Blois.'

So, the threat had come. It was no more than she had been expecting, but still there flashed into her mind a stab of bitter resentment, that always, men dictated to her. *Arrogant beast*, thought Marie, but she bit her lower lip and said nothing. Neither did Henri speak again until the carriage reached the house. Their conversational exchanges were generally of this nature, she reflected. He issued instructions and she was expected to obey them. A mistress was not for talking to, at least, not seriously, though she was expected to take part in absurd ribaldry with her lover's friends. She thought again in what little time there was left of the journey home, of the one man who had been interested in her mind. Although, as she reminded herself, he had strongly objected to her mind developing a taste for writers such as Voltaire and Pascal.

The extensive library of the comte's home in Paris, wholly neglected by its owner, had been Marie's solace since she had arrived in the city. She devoured books whenever the opportunity arose, as one obsessed with a determination to continue an education which had been belated in its start, but which had given her the most profound satisfaction in her short life. Unfortunately, the opportunities occurred too rarely, for the comte had what she considered to be a completely irrational dislike of his mistress reading. He told her he found it "unfitting". It was for her body that he had brought her to Paris, he reminded her. He wasn't aware that the delights of lovemaking could include anything called "the library position", he added, with coarse humour. Yet in this matter she dared to obey him, to drug herself with reading.

All too quickly they arrived. The house was ablaze with light and the company already assembled in the salon. Some thirty people were gathered around the supper table, which was wonderfully decked with bouquets of golden roses and twining delphiniums, set in a row down the middle. There were purple linen napkins in glasses, folded to resemble bishops' mitres. A bold-eyed, dark-haired courtesan laughed raucously as she perceived the joke, and, whisking a napkin from one of the glasses, she placed it on her lover's head. Laughter filled the room, warm with a scent compounded of the flowers and the women's perfume and the savour of fine foods. How wonderfully elegant it was, with the reds and pinks of the wine, gleaming in the candlelight and harmonising with the platters of frilled prawns. Beautifully dressed pheasants, still with their green and gold tail feathers, were piled in mounds. Luscious fruits were arranged in open baskets lined with moss, beside delicate pastries filled with chocolate and cream, piled in a tower, to resemble a chateau. Solemn faced servants, in silk stockings and gold knee breeches, handed the food to the guests, who ate little but drank much, toasting themselves from each other's' glasses as a preliminary to the important business of lovemaking.

The Comte de Blois cast a swift glance of greeting to his guests and surveyed the room; his credit in fashionable Paris greatly depended on the quality of his food and wine and the charms of the mistress he kept. But the proof of his credit was to be found in the company he could muster to appreciate his possessions. He was pleased. Taking the arm of his mistress, he sauntered through the room, smiling graciously at his guests and exchanging pleasantries, until he reached his target, a tall, square, heavily built man, wearing an exaggeratedly fashionable evening coat with enormous buttons of coloured stone. Henri bowed low before embarking on his speech to his guest.

'It is an immense joy to me and my household that you should honour our establishment this evening, my dear Comte. May I present to you my little friend, Marie Gouze, fresh from the country one might say, although her freshness is a little ripened by my loving attentions, I trust.' He simpered at his own witticism before continuing, 'Marie, I have the honour to present to you the Comte Honore Gabriel Riquetti de Mirabeau, under whose obligation we feel ourselves to be, very greatly, in honouring our soiree with his presence.' Finishing this polite address to turned to Marie and continued, 'You, my dear, will be pleased to entertain the Comte and help him to a little refreshment, will you not?' He gripped her arm above the elbow as he spoke.

'Certainly sir,' whispered Marie, as she gazed in amazement at the ugly, pock-marked face of the visitor, crowned by an exaggerated mass of curled and powdered hair. His unnaturally protuberant eyes were full of fire as he looked down at her, slowly, lasciviously. His reply was addressed not to her, but to his host;

'I congratulate you, my dear Henri, on the flower you have picked in the country. The fragrance is most sweet and refreshing and I shall be pleased to savour it awhile.'

Marie, in her short time in Paris, had become accustomed to her lover's style of reference to her as a chattel, although she resented it nonetheless. She simply replied, 'What would you care to eat, Monsieur Le Comte de Mirabeau?'

'It is what I should care to enjoy for dessert which interests me most, at this moment, my dear.'

'Just at present this little peach is bespoken, remember, my good friend,' rejoined her lover, savouring the experience of dangling his mistress before his illustrious guest.

'So! What does the lady savour herself, I wonder?' asked Mirabeau, smiling at her. Despite his ugly appearance his reputation for charm was not unfounded.

'The little lady claims a dislike for eating flesh, so she tells me,' said the Comte de Blois, 'but we are teaching her to respond a little better to our tastes.' So saying, he picked a pink prawn from the dish beside him and, without pausing to remove the shell, parted her lips with his fingers and thrust the whiskery head between her teeth.

Filled with rage and nausea, Marie spat the shell from her mouth and fled from the room. The habits and manners of the fashionable world of Paris repelled her. Yet here she was, penniless and friendless, except for the protection of the young lord she was beginning to despise and whose protection was clearly ephemeral. In reality, there was little to choose between Louis Aubry and the aristocratic young lord with whom she had thrown in her lot. She had made a mistake, as Father Michel had warned her. But there was no way back. She was too much disgraced, and too proud, to return to her home, She must, somehow, establish a life for herself in Paris. She felt dreadfully alone and in need of advice. Father Michel had always been her confessor and adviser, even though she had frequently disregarded his advice and disobeyed him. But she felt the need for a mentor. Probably she would never see Father Michel again. Her dilemma and her misery overwhelmed her. There was a new sense of panic. With tears streaming down her cheeks, she rushed from the scene of her humiliation in the salon, and sought the refuge of the library. There she kicked off her silk shoes and curled up on the couch. She knew she had secreted Voltaire's *Candide* beneath the gold damask cushions. She had read it many times, but she never tired of doing so, for each time she felt she understood more. Besides, the absurd fantasies of *Candide* allowed her to escape from the grim reality of Parisian life. Life in Paris was even more artificial, she thought, without being meaningful in any way that she had yet discovered. She lost herself in the unreality of Westphalia.

Candide was so amusing! So many wildly impossible and absurd catastrophes happened to the young adventurer, any mortal must surely have died of despair, if not from the reversals of fortune itself. And yet throughout all, Dr Pangloss remained so delightfully, so irrationally optimistic! The corruption of the real world slipped away from Marie as unobtrusively as footprints disappear from the shore at the flow of the tide. She was living in the world of Voltaire's eccentric philosopher, who firmly believed that everything was for the best, in the best of all possible worlds.

Mirabeau heard her tinkling laughter as he walked along the passage; he was in search of her. In truth he had been a little disgusted at the crude behaviour of young Henri de Blois, to what was obviously a very young and very naive mistress, and he had left the room immediately after the little scene. He prided himself on his skill in wooing women, not intimidating them. He opened the door noiselessly and smiled gently at the little figure curled up on the couch. 'Something amuses you, *mademoiselle*? I am glad that is so.'

'I did not think to be disturbed here, Monsieur le Comte' replied Marie defensively. 'Merely, I am reading.'

'May I enquire your taste in books?' Without waiting for her reply, he took the book quietly from her hands and scrutinized the cover. 'Voltaire!' He looked at her closely, his interest visibly increasing. 'May I enquire what attracts so young a lady to so great a master of the literary arts? You are to be congratulated on your taste.'

Despite herself, Marie was flattered and answered ingenuously.

'Well, many things, Monsieur Mirabeau. Apart from *Candide,* I have been so impressed by his response to Pascal, that the question of the existence of God is not a wager, but the enquiry of persons who doubt and ask to be enlightened. It is too important a matter to be the subject of a bet.' She continued on a sober note, 'I too have doubted, and wished to know. It would have been greatly in my interest, to truly believe in God, for then I could have entered the convent in all honesty. But, as Voltaire has said, my interest in believing a thing is not a proof of the existence of that thing.'

Mirabeau was astonished. He looked at her intently. She was greatly altered, he thought, when she forgot her fear and spoke naturally. She displayed a quite remarkable native intelligence. She was, moreover, very beautiful. He sat down beside her.

'And so,' Marie continued, warming to her theme, 'I have read everything written by Monsieur Voltaire, that has come my way. But this is still my favourite, for it is so amusing! She picked up *Candide* and moved closer to her companion, to point to the place where she had been reading.

'See here, this is where you heard me laughing. It was because Pangloss would persuade us that when tragedies happen, even the great earthquake at Lisbon, it must be for a purpose, for nothing God does is without purpose. The harbour at Lisbon must have been made on purpose for the Anabaptist to drown there, says Pangloss. It is so absurd! Yet, it is hopeful, despite everything.'

Mirabeau looked at her narrowly and asked mildly, 'Do you think that is what Voltaire is really saying?'

Marie frowned and thought before replying, 'Well, not really. No, in fact I think his meaning is something quite different. I think he is making a mockery of what the church would have us believe about the good which comes from suffering. He could not be serious in what he writes.'

Mirabeau raised his eyebrows. He rose from the couch and made a low bow to her. 'Bravo, *ma chere!* Your understanding is most apt. Voltaire is no lover of the church and has long aroused its enmity by ridiculing and satirising its authoritarian rule. Here, he is lampooning religious belief. He despises the false optimism which is no satisfactory answer to the problem of evil.'

Marie, nodded, intrigued by his judgement. 'I had thought so,' she added, demurely, I thank you, Monsieur Le Comte, for the help you have given me in understanding this piece.'

'Who taught you to read?' he asked, his interest now thoroughly aroused.

'The priest in the village where I was born. He was my very good friend.'

Mirabeau's eyebrows rose again. This young lady was certainly full of surprises.

'Your friend the priest surely did not approve of Voltaire?'

'No,' she agreed. 'he did not. However, at the time I did not quite understand why. He taught me to read, yes, for I begged him to do so, and he had befriended me as a small child.' She gave Mirabeau a wicked little smile and continued, 'He was unable to direct my taste in profession, as well as my taste in reading.'

He smiled back at her: 'So it is to be seen. Yet, if I may say so, you are rather an unusual young lady to have embarked on the life of a courtesan. What made you do so? Did you perhaps suffer a disappointment with your friend the priest? He was your lover, I imagine?'

'No, indeed! His advice to me was to enter the church as a sister in the Ursuline Convent. I could not bring myself to tell him, truly, of my want of faith. He was not my lover; have I not told you, he is a priest? I had no lover, other than my husband, until I came here to Paris. And the title, *lover,* ill befits Louis Aubry or Henri de Blois!' she added, bitterly.

Mirabeau bowed again, but answered, sardonically, 'I beg your pardon, *ma chere*. It would not be as unusual as you imagine, for a priest of the church to undertake your education in matters aside from literature. But I certainly crave your pardon for my misunderstanding.'

Marie shook her head, troubled once more. 'It is no

matter. Simply, I did not imagine such things to be possible.'

'If you will forgive my intrusiveness once more, my dear young lady, it seems that there are a number of matters you do not properly understand about the life you have embarked upon, judging from the little scene I witnessed between you and Henri, in the salon. You are unusually clever, in matters of the intellect. But that does not befit you to become a successful courtesan, if I may say so.'

'I know it,' Marie replied sadly, brushing a tear impatiently from her cheek. 'I do not know what to do. I am afraid.'

He raised her from the couch and took her small heart-shaped face between the palms of his hands. 'Do not be afraid,' came his determined reply. 'I will help you.'

1772 Mirabeau

Here was a new adventure for Honore Gabriel Riquetti de Mirabeau. As a young man, his sexual appetite was voracious and his palate required constant titillation. This would be a different kind of love affair, he thought, perhaps not a sexual affair at all, though that was unlikely, for he had always made love to as many women as could be persuaded to go to his bed. Their number was considerable, for despite his ugliness he had immense charm. He was intelligent, outrageous, provocative and vain, yet he was nevertheless very kind. In truth, he had a genuine desire to help the young courtesan who had attracted his fancy for the rather unusual reason that she appeared to have a mind of her own. He scorned the behaviour of many of his contemporaries when it came to affairs of the heart. Men such as Henri de Blois would frighten off so nervous a creature. The young fool lacked the wit to appreciate the rarity of the little fawn who had come into his path. It would be a pleasure to instruct her, he was sure.

And so it proved to be. Marie, installed in the house of the Comte de Mirabeau, immediately felt secure and, in a short space of time, became very grateful for his kindness. Although he was not very much older than her, he acted as her mentor, as Father Michel had done. But the course of instruction was very different. It was, he said with almost brotherly affection, as he seated her on his knee and talked to her, a series of lessons in the most profitable and enjoyable profession in the world. All she had to do was learn a little sense about this notion of love, and learn to exploit the great gifts God had given her — without guilt.

'You see, Marie, we must all use our God given assets to their greatest advantage. You have been born poor, a grave disadvantage in any age. But you have also been born a woman, and very beautiful. You have had the good sense to realise that this combination of assets can enable you to overcome your poverty, and yet you shrink from doing so. Why is this, do you think?'

Marie frowned, then replied, 'It is because of the teaching of the church, that what I do is sinful.'

'Quite correct, my dear. And I doubt not that you have been peculiarly affected by your association with this priest you speak of. In all honesty, my dear, he sounds a sanctimonious prig, and his holiness a little suspect, given his great interest in you.'

'No, no indeed,' she replied, rising from his lap and pacing around the room in agitation. 'He is a good man. He loves me.'

'He is nevertheless deluded, as are all who remain under the sway of the church, or pretend to be. The church is no friend to women, Marie, but perpetuates an attitude to them first engendered by the absurd story of Eve. You, who have read Voltaire's writing, should know how he viewed the church, as a hotbed of intolerance. In Voltaire's eyes, a man's religion is his own honest views about the Universe, and the possible existence of God. Given that it is impossible to prove by reason, either that God exists or He does not, no one has the right to dictate to another, what he should believe, or whether he should believe in anything at all. Perhaps the Universe just *is*. But above all, Marie, forget the church's notions of love. Forget them, most certainly, where the bedchamber is concerned. In this world in which we live, in French society under the Bourbons, love has little to do with marriage. We marry for practical and dynastic reasons. And yet the church would have it that love within marriage is the only love which may be permitted. All vanity and nonsense! Think instead of love as an amusing recreation, as a pastime which, in your case can be wonderfully lucrative.'

'It is not easy to do so,' she whispered.

'No one suggests that it is easy, Marie. When you first tried to read, at the knees of your charming priest, I doubt not that you experienced difficulties. You overcame them, as you can overcome these.'

'Would that I had not been born a woman!' she cried. 'Would that there were other ways to be independent!'

'Well, my dear, there are not,' he replied bluntly. 'Not as society is at present arranged.'

'I pray that it may not always be so!' she cried.

'Pray, by all means, my dear,' he answered mildly, 'but for the present I beg of you to adopt a practical solution, as our esteemed Voltaire would advise. There is much solace to be found by leading a good and useful life, in the hope that there is at the last some ultimate justice in the Universe. Now what could be better or more useful than the services you will be able to provide, if you will only take a little trouble to perfect them?' He placed his hands on her shoulders, and, lifting her chin, kissed her gently on the lips. Obediently, Marie responded to his embrace.

'That is a little better, Marie,' he said with satisfaction. 'You are becoming a model pupil, though there is yet more to learn.'

'And what would you have me learn?' she asked, smiling coquettishly.

'We must take, as I have said, practical steps,' he replied, very seriously, as he led her to the bedchamber.

Several weeks later, Marie, dressed in a frilled wrapper, sat on the balcony with Mirabeau, breakfasting on coffee and white rolls. They resumed their conversation on the accustomed lines of tutor and pupil, he naturally taking the lead.

'It is most important, my dear, that you rid your mind of foolish notions of love, as I have explained. Have you done so?'

'Certainly sir,' she replied meekly.

'As regards myself, most particularly?'

'Naturally, since you have so instructed me,' she replied.

Despite himself, he experienced a moment's regret. Nevertheless, it was genuinely his desire to accomplish the interesting task he had set himself, so he continued speaking in his usual authoritarian way.

'I am most ambitious, my dear, as regards the heights you may attain. Given your beauty and charm, you may do considerably better than oafs such as Henri of Blois. Indeed, it is my belief that your unfortunate affair with him, and of course, the rather morbid attitude you developed as a result of your beloved priest's beliefs, have been much to blame for your initial difficulties with the arts of love.'

He is jealous of my love for Father Michel, she thought, but said nothing.

'Yes, indeed, given your natural talents and your great beauty, there is no reason why you should not aspire to the highest in the land, the great Bourbons, even,' Mirabeau continued, meditatively.

'The king!' she replied, astonished.

'Yes, why not? Others have done so, although in truth it would be difficult to arrange a liaison just at present. Louis, he who was called "The Well–Beloved" by the people, is enamoured of a new mistress, Madame Du Barry, who possesses not a quarter of your charms, my dear, though she is infinitely your superior in the skills of capitalising on her position. And the dauphin is made of rather different metal from his grandfather, our beloved monarch. He who will become Louis XV1 has been much influenced by his mother and his gruesome-looking aunts. He has been taught to believe that pretty women are a temptation to sin. Who knows but that in time he may prove to be a rarity among his family, a faithful husband!' Mirabeau laughed aloud at the mere idea of such an oddity seated upon the throne of France.

'I like the sound of the dauphin,' retorted Marie. 'He sounds like a good man.'

'Good perhaps, but goodness is not enough, especially in the times in which we live. You should instead admire his grandfather, our present king, who has done much, with his notorious love affairs, to further the ambitions and prospects of women such as yourself. In truth, the dauphin is a weak and boorish creature who is as likely to prove impotent as he is to be a good husband. More importantly, I do not believe he is equal to the task of reforming the monarchy, and that, I assure you, will be necessary in our lifetime, Marie.'

'Why so?' she enquired, fascinated by the turn the conversation had taken.

Mirabeau shrugged, 'As you so often point out, my dear, there are gross inequalities and injustices in this world, and I believe the time is coming when the people will try to redress them. Unlike our good Voltaire, I believe we need the monarchy as an anchor for the people, or something worse could yet befall them. But the Bourbons are unlikely to perceive the need for change, I fear.'

'It must be wonderful to be a princess of the blood!' exclaimed Marie, rapturously.

'There speaks a certain inconsistency in your stance, if I may say so, Marie, for you are in all probability the poor little by-blow of our aristocrats' tendencies to ravish the poor and leave no provision for the bastard children who are the results. You should have no love for the aristocracy of this land, but should instead seek to exploit them.'

'It is true that I have no love for such injustice,' replied Marie.

'Then let us return to the practical task of instructing you in the only way to overcome the present injustices of your position, Marie. Forget your romantic attachment to the monarchy. What is vital, my dear, is that you appreciate the need to accumulate money.'

'*Bien sur!* Is that not obvious?'

'Obvious as it may seem, Marie, I have known courtesans to be remarkably careless of this simple fact of life. They acquire the most luxurious apartments, they learn to play at cards, they bedeck themselves with jewels which do nothing to add to their charms. Before they realise what they are about, they find themselves unable to live on an income of less than a hundred thousand francs a year and are forced to take three or four lovers at a time in order to keep the bailiffs from the door. Hence they ruin their attractions early, by overindulgence, just to maintain an extravagant lifestyle. Take my advice, Marie, when I presently establish you in your own apartments, with the lover who is already burning to make your acquaintance. Look to the example of Madame Du Barry. It is possible to become a rich woman. But only if you live cautiously.'

'You already have a new lover in mind?' Marie asked, in some trepidation.

'Yes, most certainly. My friend Jacques Bietrix de Rozieres is anxious to meet you. He comes from Lyon and is a wealthy man, a military transport entrepreneur. He is cultivated. He will be able to introduce you into artistic and philosophical *salons,* where you will meet people who will amuse and interest you. Women such as Madame de Montesson and the Comtesse de Beauharnais, who are aspiring writers, with the literary interests you share. It will be a wonderful opportunity for you, but, alas, a sad regret for me.'

'You will regret my leaving?'

'*Bien sur.* to use your own words, Marie, that is obvious. But as I have said so frequently, we must be practical. To be frank with you, my dear, I cannot afford to keep you for long. Delightful though our little experience has been, it must necessarily be short-lived. I myself have not always followed the good advice I have given you. My debts are enormous and the only way to discharge them will be through marriage with some extremely rich, but no doubt extremely plain, daughter of a nobleman who will overlook my reputation for the sake of my lineage. Such is the way of the world. One must live, and to live it is necessary to acquire money. So you see Marie, our cases are not so very different. Love has nothing to do with us.'

'So I am beginning to realise,' she responded dolefully. He caught the note of sadness in her voice and, in truth, it pleased his vanity that she should be sorry to leave his establishment. Nevertheless, he replied cheerfully,

'Come, there is no need to repine, Marie. In truth, your position is rather more favourable than mine. De Rozieres will treat you well, and as I have said, he has the *entree* to circles where you will find much to enjoy. All you have to do is provide him with the charms of the bedchamber, as you are learning to do so well. As for the future, who knows? With care and frugality you may one day be able to afford to take the lover of your own choosing, while I shall be tied for life to a dull and nagging wife.'

'Will you be unfaithful to her?' she asked, curiously.

'Certainly, if the opportunity presents itself, and I doubt not that it will.'

'I am sure it will, she replied. 'For a nobleman such as yourself, it is to be expected. I doubt not that your "plain, well-born wife" will passively accept her lot, for she will be your chattel, while you will be free. In which case, your prospects in life are still better than mine. I thank you for all your care and kindness, Monsieur le Comte. You have been a good friend to me and I shall not forget your advice when we come to part.

I doubt not that you are right about most things, but in one respect you are wrong. I shall never be able to take the lover of my choice.'

1783 Father Michel's Story

I think I was always destined to be a priest; I cannot remember a time when I did not know my vocation was to serve God. I was a fastidious child, very particular about washing my face and hands, especially my hands. I liked always to be clean. I can remember my mother watching me and smiling; she would say, 'Those are priest's hands.' She was a very holy woman, very pious and devout. She was always dressed with great neatness and propriety, with her housedress buttoned up tightly to her chin, and with a shawl draped over her shoulders. She was devoted to the Virgin Mother and the saints, especially the female saints, such as Saint Catherine of Siena. I can remember her reading me the stories of their lives, although I cannot recall the exact details. As a child I would play a game, pretending I was a priest. I would wash my hands carefully and take small morsels of bread and the dregs of the wine from the carafe. Then I would "play priest" while my mother watched, nodding her head and looking at me, very wisely, very lovingly. My father I do not remember at all, nor do I remember anyone telling me about him.

So I suppose that when I entered the seminary I was simply fulfilling what I had always wanted. Celibacy came easily for me. I would pray to God to give me strength to resist temptation, but in all honesty, I hardly knew what that meant. As I say, I had a dislike of the body and all its functions. I did not like the idea of being "manly". It seemed too coarse, too uncouth. When I was first ordained I remember the ecstasy of serving Mass, the great joy and privilege, that mine were the hands which would transform the sacred elements into the Body and Blood of Christ. So it was important to keep myself spotless, not only in the soul, but in the body as well. I must keep my hands clean. I have always done so. As time has passed, the Mass has become more of a ritual; the ecstasy has gone, but the duty remains. But to perform this duty, it is still necessary to observe scrupulous cleanliness.

Marie Gouze came into my life many years ago, when she was a seven-year-old child, She was beautiful then and she is beautiful now, even though many years have passed and she is thirty-five years old. She visits this small country parish every year, at least twice a year, bringing her son Pierre with her. Often he stays for a few months, but she always returns to Paris. Her life is spent in the city now, and it is a life that I deplore, as she well knows. Still, if any human holds my heart, such feelings as I can spare from my devotion to God and his Mother, she is that person. She is the only human being who has ever been given my consecrated hands to hold. When we walk and talk in the meadows, we still walk hand in hand. It is the only human contact I have ever had or have ever wanted. Simply, her presence is like the sun coming from behind a cloud. She lights up the world, and everything is gaiety and gladness. When she is gone the world turns grey.

Her life now is deplorable, as I have said. I wish she would let me hear her confession. She says that is impossible, hypocritical, for she has no intention of leaving her "profession" as a high-class courtesan. Therefore, she says, how can she say she repents of sins which she has every intention of committing again? For a woman, she is devastatingly logical in her thinking, and I blame myself, bitterly, that it was I who taught her to read. Of course, I could not know that her reading would lead her so far astray, in proper womanly behaviour. Still, I would like to be her confessor. It would no doubt be shocking and dreadful, to hear the details of her fornications with men — and there have been many. It would be my duty to listen to such details and, with my dislike of all things carnal, I think it would be very painful. But then it would also be my duty to give her penance and I should like that duty, painful though it would be, especially for her. I remember once giving her a penance which required bodily chastisement. On that occasion, it was entirely necessary to expose her flesh. I confess that her body was very beautiful. But I did not touch it with my hands of course, I used a switch. And I did not see her entirely naked. Long ago, Marie told me that she saw a painting called *Le Bon Jugement de Paris* in the Chateau Le Vigin. A naked man, Paris, is judging which of the three goddesses, Venus, Minerva, or Juno, is the most beautiful. She has since told me that this painting, originally by Rubens, is reproduced in many grand houses of people of the nobility, in Paris, so that men may gaze at women's bodies. She was very flippant, even cynical, when she spoke of it.

'Most men like to look at naked women, Father Michel.' And then she asked, 'Do you?' But of course I could not answer such a question. I shall never see a naked woman in a painting, or in the flesh.

As I said, her son Pierre usually comes to Pont d'Herault

when she makes her visits. I remember him since the day of his birth, even before his mother took notice of him, for she was ill with puerperal fever after he was born. Apart from the child's grandmother, mine were the first hands to hold him. I remember he looked like a beautiful bronze cherub, wriggling and squalling, when I had washed the repulsive stains of childbirth from him. For the first four years of his life he lived in the village, with his mother and grandmother. He was a child who seemed to be greatly attracted to mud and grime. He would roll in the mud; always he seemed to be covered in mud, even if it had not rained for a week. He would roll in the cow dung and suck warm milk from the cow's teats, as if he remembered how his grandmother had fed him as an infant. In winter he would fall asleep on the straw intended for the cows' bedding. I made great efforts to cure him of his propensity for grime, for it distressed me greatly. I would drag him to the pump and wash him thoroughly. Of course, I could not wash his entire body, once he had passed infancy. That would have been unseemly, since I have a high respect for the privacy of the body. But his face, hair and hands were given a most thorough washing. How the layers of grime were cleansed away, under my ministrations! His hair was the worst, for it was a veritable nest of particles of earth and stones and lice. At last he would emerge, spluttering and crying. I would watch him race around with aimless, animal gusto, as the sun dried his bronze-gold curls, a little darker than those of his mother. He looked like one of the cupids in the painted scenes of God in his Heaven.

Before Marie took him to Paris I had embarked on teaching him his lessons. It had been a mistake to teach his mother to read, but here was a boy-child, of dubious lineage. He should have the rudiments of learning. But he was not like his mother, who had thirsted for knowledge as a child. He was a reluctant pupil. I am inclined to believe Marie in her conviction that his grandsire was of high birth, and a scholar. But if this is so, the grandson has not inherited his intellect. He would sit on my knee as I attempted to teach him his letters, and the catechism. Prodigious yawns of boredom would begin, not ten minutes after we had begun. Then he would squirm and wriggle and make horrible grimaces. He would kick and scream and eventually struggle away and race off to the cowshed.

I have despaired of having any influence with Pierre, now he is seventeen years old. I have every reason to believe that, when he visits Pont d'Herault, he has carnal knowledge of the village girls. He is, in every respect, a most unsatisfactory young man. Marie tells me he is destined for the army, that, under the patronage of her friend, Jacques Beatrix de Rozieres, he will enter *L'Ecole Militaire* in Paris. I suppose that will be a suitable destiny for him, since, to my sorrow, I know that he has pronounced bestial tendencies. Unlike his mother, who remains fair and charming, despite the depraved life she lives. She tells me she does not love Jacques Beatrix de Rozieres, her present "protector". He is wealthy and amiable, but she declares that she does not love him, that she has never loved any of them. They are, she says, a means to an end, and that the end she desires is to expose and write about the evils of poverty and oppression, especially the oppression of women. Nowadays she calls herself Olympe de Gouges, but to me she will always be my Marie.

Time passes quickly for me. With one day so like another, with no change from year to year, except for the joyous interludes when Marie visits Pont d'Herault, time passes with monotonous speed. The fine weather, the sun and rain to nurture and ripen the crops in the cycle of yearly seasons, these I think of as the greatest gifts God can give to man. There is comfort in monotony. I say Mass very early, I walk in the meadows and in winter I retire early to my fireside. There I read the Lives of the Saints and the Holy Scriptures, by candle and firelight. I find solace in the thought that it matters not, in this short and transitory life, if one sometimes feels empty and barren. In the long days that are friendless and grey, I think of the glory of my final hour, when I shall see the radiance of God and all his angels.

Once I had a short vacation and left my parish for a walking tour in the higher hills. It was a solitary vacation, of course, for so is all my life. I do not have human contact. I remember that when I started out it was a beautiful day, with great clusters of snowy clouds in an azure sky. Then, suddenly, the clouds thickened and turned grey. The sun went behind a cloud and a light rain began to fall. I walked on alone, listening to the sound of the crickets chirping in the long grass. Then I came to a waterfall, and as the water cascaded down it seemed to form a high wall, stretching up to the heavens. Then the sun came out suddenly from behind the clouds and everything seemed to be motionless as I saw the glorious colours of the rainbow behind the glistening wall of water. It was a most remarkable experience. It was as if God had set His bow in the sky to send me a message, as He did to the prophet, Noah. But all I could think about was the beauty of the rainbow and the beauty of Marie Gouze.

1784 Pierre's Story

It was a strange childhood, two different childhoods, really. It was as if I was a child in two different worlds, not a member of the third estate and not a nobleman either. I have a mother who has become a notorious courtesan, and no father to give me a name. In France it is usual to be aware of one's position in life. The first and second estates of the land are the church and clergy and the nobility. (Of course, it is well to be born a nobleman but it defeats my understanding why anyone should choose to become a priest; it is a calling I despise.) Mind you, it is possible to rise to a high position in the church, but only if one has wealth and breeding. I have neither. The third estate is the mass of people, the common folk. Well, I am not one of them, but my father is dead and my grandfather, reputed to be a marquis, has never claimed my mother as his own. It gives a man a sense of unease, not knowing who he is. In France, name and position are of great importance. I am merely Pierre Aubry, although I am also known as Pierre Aubry de Gouges, taking the name my mother has adopted.

I also find it rather difficult to describe my feelings for my mother. As a small child I adored her, she seemed so beautiful, a small, rustling creature, smelling of herbs and flowers. I remember liking the way she smelled and hoping she would pick me up so I could bury my head in the scent. She seemed to do so a lot when I was very small. Then, when I was four years old, we came to Paris, and I saw her less often. She was like an exotic butterfly, flitting into my room. Then she would flash her wings and disappear, just like a butterfly. Now and then we would walk together in the Tuileries Garden. I remember one occasion when she was wearing a gown the colour of lavender; I clearly remember thinking it was like the colours of the evening sky. She smelled of lavender too. On that walk she suddenly stopped and stooped down and took my face in her hands, scrutinising me closely. There was a small crease of vexation between her brows and the great flashing rings on her fingers dug into my jaw bone as she stared at me. She shook her head as if she was disappointed in what she saw, though I don't remember her actually saying anything. She seemed more vexed, I think, about the dirt that had got on to the hem of her gown. It is my belief that I reminded her of my father. She never spoke of him at all but provided me with "uncles" instead. There have been many of them and, in general they have been indifferent to my existence. My mother, on the other hand, claims to adore me. She says I am the great joy of her life, but I don't believe her. She is given to making exaggerated claims. For all I know, she might have invented the story of her own noble birth, and the rejection of her real father. As I grew up, I was never entirely sure the story was true, or whether it was the invention of my mother's distorted imagination.

If anyone is a joy in her life it is Father Michel Dupre, a simple country priest who lives in the village near Montauban, where she was born. For some unfathomable reason she visits him often, ostensibly to see her mother and half brothers and sisters. I vaguely remember him before we came to live in

Paris, fussing over me if I was dirty and bothering me with book learning. He was a bore and a fusspot then and he is still. There is something reserved and effeminate about him that unnerves me. What my mother sees in him is beyond me. I despise the whole race of the priesthood as fools and hypocrites. But my mother still likes to walk and talk with him, when she visits the country. When I was growing up she would often leave me in Pont d'Herault for a few weeks, at my grandmother's house. I think it got me out of her way, while she was entertaining her lovers. That is why I say I had two different childhoods, for my grandmother was very poor and, frankly, a very common old woman. Yet I was fond of her, she was a jolly, carefree sort of person and it was good to be among my half-uncles and aunts for a while. They were playmates for me, for some of them were scarcely older than I. In Paris my life was very different, far grander of course, but rather solitary. I had no companions of my own age, only boring tutors.

As I have grown older I must say I prefer the girls in the country. They are far easier to seduce than Parisian women and make no fuss if you throw them down in the hay, hoist up their petticoats and bid them raise their legs high in the air. Then I give them a good pounding; I learned quite early how to do so and now I ram it home hard. Sometimes I turn them over and give them a good pasting on the buttocks with my riding crop; they deserve it, the sluts. I like to take them from behind too, with their heads down, turned sideways like poor sheep's heads in the straw, so I can see their silly faces. Then I make sure their behinds are well raised before I let them have it. *Bien sur,* the girls in the country are very much to my taste, and for the time being it is good sport. Of course it will be a different matter when I come to marry. Then it will be necessary to seek a woman of breeding. There is much to do before then, to further my career. My mother tells me that, under the patronage of her "friend" de Rozieres, I can expect to enter *L'Ecole Militaire* and take up a career as a soldier. Soldiering appeals to me, and of course I have the need to better myself.

I suppose I should be grateful to my mother for the advantages she seeks for me. It is not that I mind, really, her profession as a courtesan. After all, a woman is meant to be kept in the bedchamber, it is what she is for. My real objection is that my mother does not confine herself to her chosen profession. She has begun to meddle in affairs which are of no concern of hers, and which she cannot possibly understand. Why, she tells me she has just written a play against slavery, called *Zamore and Mirza!* What can she possibly know of such things and why should she concern herself with the conditions of the lower classes? Furthermore, these are only black people! She makes herself ridiculous, and worse, she may get herself into trouble and that will mean trouble for anyone who bears her name. As I said, it is the great pity of my life that I have no real name.

Once my mother and I went to Pont d'Herault on the occasion of my grandmother's funeral. In truth, I felt some sadness. She was old, but I had been fond of her; she was more a mother to me than her daughter had been and I had many good memories of times at her house. The day of the funeral was one of those grey days; the rain grizzled drearily in the sky and great leaden clouds gathered overhead as we carried the coffin. It was heavy going, our boots squelched through the mud as we carried her towards the bottom of the burial ground, where a grave had already been dug in the grass. The black pall covering the coffin was drenched like some miserable black crow; I remember the doleful sound of it dripping as we moved ponderously forward in a series of jerks, as if we were on a boat being tossed by every wave. The ropes were placed in position and the coffin was pushed onto them. I watched it go down, down into the bowels of the earth with my grandmother within. Then there was a thud and the ropes came creaking up again. Father Michel was officiating but I wasn't really listening as he recited his mumbo-jumbo over the coffin. I was struck by one of the mourners standing huddled in his cloak on the other side of the grave, an old man bent over a walking stick.

I recognised him as a local nobleman, the Marquis Lefranc de Pompignan, although I had never had occasion before to speak to him. It struck me as rather strange, his being one of the mourners. Generally, the nobility have little or nothing to do with the ordinary people, apart from exacting their dues and tithes from them. Father Michel, his cassock flapping around his legs in the gale, at last finished his mutterings and stooped to pick up a clod of earth to sprinkle on the coffin. His womanish hands repelled me; they were all covered in clay. So I did not follow suit. What was the point anyway? I stepped over to the old man instead, to thank him for his attentions to my grandmother, in coming to her interment. I'll never forget his reply, or the cunning look on his grizzled old face as he said,

'We were related, in a manner. She was the mother of my child. And you, my boy, must be *grand-fils* to me. *Quelle idée! C'est amusant, n'est-ce pas?*'

I could not take in his meaning at first. I thought the old man was demented, and who could blame me? And it took a good deal more explanation before I wrenched the whole story out of him although, truth to tell, he was more than willing to tell me of my antecedents. He positively revelled in the details of his relations with my grandmother, and the siring of my mother, the old lecher. It was a case of reliving old conquests, I suppose.

The marquis did not speak to my mother and she studiously ignored his presence. She has recently taken to writing of the evils of men who do not acknowledge their bastard children and leave them without monetary provision. She is passionate in her defence of the rights of illegitimate children. Well, I take her point, after all, the matter concerns me. I am his grandson and I am nameless. But my feelings were strangely mixed on that day, and so they remain. The story of my mother's birth was true, after all. But I can't honestly say I blame the old lecher. As I have said, I am a red-blooded man myself. It has always been an understood thing, that the nobility should have the first pickings of the village women. That is the way it has always been and, as for the women, it's not to be expected they would have any say in the matter, is it? The trouble with my mother is that she seems to think she should interfere in these matters. She meddles in affairs which are no concern of hers, and this, I predict, will lead her into trouble. My great wish is that she does not drag me into her difficulties, for I am merely Pierre Aubry de Gouges.

Part Two

1789 The Revolution

There was a conspiratorial murmur among the fishwives of Les Halles in the early morning of October 3rd 1789, quite unlike the strident yelling and raucous laughter that usually accompanied the setting out of their wares. Outwardly, everything was as usual; wicker baskets revealed stiff, mottled mackerel and conger eel, knotted and twisted together like iridescent blue ropes. The knights of the sea, the salmon, were displayed separately on flat platters, their exquisitely-shaped silvery scales gleaming in the weak autumn sunlight. Mussels tumbled out of sodden sacks, pungent with the smell of sewers and seaweed. Here and there, ancient lobsters and crayfish, still living, crawled underfoot on twisted, spindly legs, looking like cantankerous giant spiders. The great blue parrot fish stared glassily from their boxes, their ugly mouths downturned and doleful, while huge flat skate, their creamy underbellies blushed with delicate pink, lay splayed out like dancers' fans. Sardines jerked and twisted their St. Vitus dance before they lay extinguished in a silvery blue mound. The great bearded pike stared malevolently, his whiskers encrusted with frost in the chill of the early morning.

Nearby, other women piled great pyramids of shiny oranges and purple grapes, while the delicate blushing skins of peaches, carefully laid in paper cases, resembled the dewy breasts of the young market women, encased in low-cut white bodices, though they wore coarse shawls over their shoulders as well, against the chilly air. At the place where the fruit and vegetable market joined the fish market, a group of women were clustered. They spoke in low voices but their whispered conversations were dangerously angry. One subject alone preoccupied them — the price of bread. It had risen during the last few weeks to swallow up more than half the weekly incomes of the poorest families.

'*Mes enfants, mes enfants,*' wailed one woman. When my little Paulette cries for bread, it hurts me here.' The young woman clutched her breast. 'I can do nothing, *je peut faire rien, rien.* And the poor child does not understand why.' She collapsed into sobs.

'Indeed, we can do nothing!' agreed another. 'While here we are, surrounded by piles of food on which the rich gorge. It is sickening!' she concluded vehemently.

'*Mais oui,* it makes me sick also, to think of them ramming the food into their slobbering mouths,' replied Brigitte Boursin, a tall, rangy woman with fanatical dark eyes, under heavily marked brows. 'So it is agreed? It is for tomorrow? We march together?'

'*Oui, Bien sur!*' came the chorus of agreement. Jeanne Souborot, a cheerful optimist with a figure like a ripe pear remarked, hopefully, 'the king will listen. He has children of his own. The queen, too, is a mother.'

'*Bien sur,* it is said they lie together now, but they did not always do so. They say the king did not father the whore's children. Only *Madame Deficit* knows who the fathers may be!'

'Or perhaps she does not know!'

'Perhaps only God knows!'

Bawdy laughter broke out from the group of women, followed by more hushed murmurings. Brigitte had the last word.

'And if he will not listen, why, we'll make him. We'll take him by the wig and drag him to Paris, that he may see how the people starve!'

The following day, a crowd of more than six thousand gathered at the Hotel de Ville, in a grey drizzle. Most of them were women. From there they set forth on the long march to Versailles. For six hours they walked, singing revolutionary songs, as the rain from the leaden sky soaked their clothes and the mud from the water-logged roads oozed into their leaking boots. But there was something exciting about that march, so many of them striding out together. The market women of Les Halles were tough, they were not accustomed to a soft life, so they marched on relentlessly, determinedly. Their rags clung to their legs and their hair flew out in dishevelled tresses; they were like a band of malevolent witches. Some nursed their infants as they tramped, others held them aloft, poor mites, thin as sparrows, living witnesses to the starvation of their mothers.

Louis XVI, returning as usual from hunting, received a deputation of women and spoke to them soothingly. He promised relief supplies would be sent to the starving capital city. He announced that he was ready to accept the Declaration of Rights drawn up by the National Assembly. but he was astounded by the demand that he should return with the women to Paris. He loathed the capital and besides, there was no precedent for such a demand. Food marches had taken place in the past, in his grandfather's time. It was customary to pacify the people. But not to be dragged to the city! When faced with a crisis, Louis was always unsure. He equivocated. He would give a reply the next day.

The women were prepared to wait. They scoured the countryside for wood and lit huge bonfires to dry their sopping clothes. As evening drew on, the main body of Parisians arrived and they all settled down for the night as best they could. Brigitte Boursin, clad only in a shift and petticoat, eased her long feet out of her boots and sat down on her cloak beside the fire. She took a long draught of vinegary wine and gazed up at the sky. It had cleared now, and was studded with stars. What a beautiful night it was; the stars were lighting the beginning of a new world, a different world from yesterday. The new day would begin the dawn of the Peoples' Republic, thought Brigitte.

Throughout the night, cries of "Liberty! Equality! Freedom!" rose like cosmic waves in the night air. The women of the campsite knitted together their spirits and their will. Their common need made them as one. Solemn vows of sisterhood were made. Never had Brigitte felt so full of love, not even when her firstborn child had lain in her arms. She loved her neighbour as herself, and that was a great deal, for she had never been so conscious of self, her purpose, her identity. She was a goddess of a fishwife as she sat and swayed with her fellow market women, now crooning, now bawling the words of their favourite songs. The red wine had made her drowsy. She lay down on the grass, cradled in the arms of another market woman, who, only four days previously, she had cursed and abused "*Le Cochon*", for underselling haddock.

At early dawn, a few hundred of the mob found a way into the Palace of Versailles. After months of starvation, their patient stoicism had evaporated. They had become as wild beasts, bent on bloody slaughter. They killed some of the royal bodyguard and nearly penetrated into the queen's apartments before they were repulsed. There could be no resistance to a mob of nearly twenty thousand people, now gathered in the streets outside the palace. In the afternoon of October 6th, the king and his family left Versailles, never to return. The triumphant procession set out on the muddy march back to Paris, led by the motley crowd of jubilant market women.

Two days later, Marie Gouze, now known in Paris as Olympe de Gouges, sat by the window of her apartment in the Rue de Rivoli, reading a pamphlet relating to these exciting events. She read quickly and feverishly, she prided herself on the speed of her reading. In the early morning light it was easy to see the crinkles at the corners of her eyes and mouth, the results of more than three decades of smiling, for she smiled a great deal. By candlelight she still passed as a beautiful woman. Many of her admirers said she always would, that she had the secret of eternal youth. There was a timeless, almost a childish quality about her looks, and she was still as slender as a sapling. At this moment she was in *dishabille,* her undressed hair tumbling about her shoulders. She clutched a rose-coloured wrapper about her naked body, the colour merged with the reddening creeper on the balcony beside the open window. The fitful autumn sun shone on the aureola of her fair hair and, with her hands clasped together in the excitement of a child anticipating a treat, she looked scarcely more than a girl.

'Honorine, *viens ici*,' she called to her maid in a flutey voice. 'Hear what has been happening here in Paris for the past two days.' She read aloud,

'A great crowd of women, many ordinary women from the market place of Les Halles, have succeeded in doing what generations of politicians have failed to do. They have brought the King of France to the capital, to be answerable to the people. Their cry for bread will not go unheeded, promised Louis XV1.'

Honorine was phlegmatic, she shrugged indifferently.

'It is nothing, madame. They are but doing what their mothers and grandmothers have done before them. It is a tradition, this, when the price of bread is high. To petition the king, I mean. My own mother...'

'But the king is in *Paris,* they say,' interrupted her mistress, impatiently ignoring Honorine's mother. Honorine refused to be moved. Often she found it part of her duties to quieten the excitement of her mistress.

'This is nothing but another bread riot, madame. Calm yourself, I beg of you.' Her words had some effect, for Olympe de Gouges frowned and considered carefully before she replied.

'No, Honorine, this is different. This is no mere riot, this is a revolution. And women are playing their part, as they should.'

Honorine's eyebrows raised and she answered sceptically,

'They say men were among the crowd, dressed as women.'

'It is possible, I suppose. No doubt the women were manipulated for political reasons. When are women not manipulated by men, for one reason or another?'

'What, madame, even you, who has men flocking for your favours, even though you choose to live retired?'

'I, more than anyone, Honorine, have been too much influenced by men. More than you can possibly know. I cannot explain.' She sat silently musing for a while, the pamphlet dropped into her lap, unheeded, while she thought of the past. Then her mood changed. She was volatile; she snatched the paper again and rose to her feet crying,

'It is of no consequence now. This year the National Constituent Assembly has declared the end of feudalism. Seigneurial rights and tithes to the church have been swept away. I have written of the enslavement of the people of the colonies, in my play *L'Esclavage des Negres,* but, in truth, the French people have also been slaves, and especially, women have been in the thrall of men. But it is past now, finished. Nothing in the past is of consequence, not in my life or in the lives of the people of France. I have need to write more! Honorine, fetch me my pen!'

Honorine stared in amazement. Her mistress must indeed be deeply moved, in the grips of an unusual excitement, since she had forgotten her morning *toilette.*

'But you are not dressed, madame!'

'Ah, no!' She smiled apologetically. 'I had forgotten. Fetch me my sky coloured silk and a lace shawl. Afterwards we must attend to the animals. And then my pen, for indeed, there is much for me to write!'

It was more than sixteen years since Marie Gouze had changed her name to Olympe de Gouges, on the advice of Mirabeau, in order to gain credibility as a courtesan and because, as the daughter of the Marquis Lefranc de Pompignan, she never forgot that a noble name was her birthright. But she was still Marie to her friends and servants in the privacy of her home in Paris, where she now lived independently. Jacques Bietrix de Rozieres had been for many years her protector, but in order to amass a fortune there were, of necessity, a number of other lovers. Her relationships with men were amicable, professional and detached. Her goal had been to achieve independence, and to further the causes of the oppressed through her writing. Since the death of her putative father, in 1784, she increasingly sought political and public recognition. Now, with the coming of great changes in France, she was sure the time was ripe for her voice to be heard.

As well as amassing a large fortune she had also acquired a strange menagerie of animals. A huge Great Dane dog, surprisingly elegant on his long legs, circled her now, gazing at her adoringly and slobbering with affection as she stood, half naked, bathing her face. She stroked his long temples, carelessly, with a wet hand. '*Voltaire, assis-toi,*' she said, gently. 'I have much to do today.' A small monkey, *Rousseau*, swung on the drapes of the peach-cushioned bed. The bed cushions had to be changed frequently, because of the droppings of the monkey, but she could not bear to part with *Rousseau*, her "hairy little man". Beside the bed, in gilded cages, sang the finches and love-birds. Marie would frequently release them, to sit upon her fingers. She would stretch out her jewelled fingers and they would sing to each other, the birds and the woman. She would croon love-songs to them, songs she had never sung to any human being, man or child. Animals were so much easier to understand than people.

The rank, sour smell of animals was masked by her flowery perfume; she sprayed herself, then dressed in the sky-blue silk and looked at herself in the glass, turning this way and that, a small frown creasing her forehead. She was dissatisfied, it was hard to say why. Honorine was accustomed to her mistress's fastidious discontent; Marie was unpredictable, rarely satisfied with her appearance, although she looked ravishing. There was a nervous irritation about her behaviour. The maid helped her to pull off the silk and produced instead a flouncy oyster coloured gown.

'Perhaps this will please you, madame?' Marie smiled ruefully,

'You are patient as always, Honorine, with my stupid whims. Indeed, there are times when I think myself very tiresome, to care for such fripperies.' She smiled and shook her head. 'Nevertheless, I cannot look a fright, not for all the revolutions in Europe! Oh, how I shall tease Father Michel when next I see him! He who said this day would never come. He has so much faith in some ways, but so little in others.'

Her relationship with the priest had been the most long lasting, and complex, of her life. Regularly, she had gone back to Pont d'Herault, ostensibly to visit her mother and take her child to see his grandmother and his aunts and uncles. In reality, as she admitted to herself, it had been to see Father Michel. In the early years there had been some bitter disagreements. She would on no account permit him to be her confessor. The act of confession was in her eyes, a hypocrisy. She had no intention of abandoning her way of life, so how could she confess? There was also a suspicion in her mind, that he had a prurient desire to hear the details of her carnal acts. She had once ventured to approach this matter, even though rather obliquely. She remembered the conversation clearly.

'Father, you cannot hear my confession. I am not repentant. This life I have chosen is the life I shall continue to live. It would be false, to confess.'

'But it is your duty to the church, to confess your sins.'

'I have told you, I consider truth more important than what you call my duty. In any case, should I change my mind and go to confession, you would be the last priest I should choose.'

'Why so, Marie?' He was confused and hurt. 'Why so, when we have been friends since your childhood, when I have loved you since then?'

'Precisely for those reasons, Father,' she had answered in measured tones. She remembered thinking carefully before she continued, 'Because what I would have to say would give you pain, and perhaps, the details of my behaviour would excite feelings in you, unbecoming to a priest.' He had refused to be drawn to her meaning and had answered stolidly.

'It would be my duty to listen to your confession, however painful to me personally.'

She was exasperated. For all seminary training, for all his piety, or perhaps in fact because of the rigours of this early experience, he was devoid of personal insight. He did not acknowledge himself to be a man, subject to the same feelings as other men. His lack of personal honesty irritated her, yet she must be generous, for she owed much to him and what he said was true, he had taught her and loved her since childhood. Therefore she had allowed the subject to lapse. But there had been other disagreements, about her child, Pierre. He had been only four years old when Marie had taken him to Paris and Father Michel had missed him sorely. He had, as he had reminded her, taken him into his care from his earliest days, washed him as a newborn child, taught him his first lessons. When they talked of this time Marie acknowledged his love for the child, whilst feeling that, as his love for her, it was doomed to disappointment.

'Pierre is a difficult child, Father Michel,' she had said, when she had returned to Pont d'Herault in 1773. Pierre was seven years old, and proving to be recalcitrant with his tutors. 'He has little inclination for study, I fear, and is often uncouth in his manners,' she continued. 'By all means, he may stay here awhile with his grandmother and you may see what you can do to improve his behaviour.'

'Marie, you speak as if you do not care for the child,' the priest responded. She had cocked her head a little on one side, as if thinking about the matter for the first time, as if she had not considered it before.

'Yes, perhaps that is so. Is it to be expected that I should? I did not want a child, after all.'

'But now he is born?'

'Inevitably, he is born. Once a woman is far gone in pregnancy there is no help for it. The child must be born. It is like... like defecation, I suppose.' She had looked at him defiantly. 'Yes, you are shocked, But I tell you, it is so. It is simply a case of there being no choice.'

'You are unnatural.'

'Unnatural! You would persuade me that it is natural to enjoy pain, such pain as no man has ever endured? It is natural to love a child whose very existence reminds you of a man you loathed? I will be unnatural all my life, if what you say is true.'

'Yet women say they love their children,' he answered

mildly.

'They say so, no doubt. I have myself told Pierre that he is the greatest joy of my life. But I fear I was not being honest. To you, Father, although I cannot tolerate the idea that you should be my confessor, I am nevertheless always truthful. Often women say they love their children because the world tells them they should do so. But what is love, anyway? Nature and society dictate that I should protect my child, that is all. It is an animal instinct and a social obligation.'

Marie's ruthless honesty, as well as her deplorable way of life, had shocked and saddened Father Michel in the early years of her life in Paris. Although she would not confess to him, she had confided that her way of life was not easy for her.

'I cannot tell you what I do, Father, for that would be an embarrassment for me and perhaps painful for you. But I will tell you how I feel. I feel nothing. It is not easy for me to be... to be responsive, you understand. I cannot respond to a man easily, despite the excellent tuition of Monsieur Le Comte de Mirabeau. There is a certain distaste, a repugnance I must always disguise.' Here was a strange idea, for the priest. Despite himself, he was intrigued.

'Marie, from what you say, it seems that celibacy would be a more fitting life for you. The life God intended.'

'That is probably so,' she agreed cheerfully. 'Alas that God did not also provide me with the means to live so! I am unfitted, I think, by temperament and inclination, to fulfill the conditions of marriage. It matters less, I believe, in the life of a courtesan. Should my lover suspect, should my coldness be too obvious, he can always terminate the affair. In fact, it rarely happens like that.' She smiled. 'I could never become a stage actress, but I can pretend nevertheless. With you, I am honest. But even with you, there are some things I hide.'

'What do you hide from me, Marie? You told me, many years ago, that you would not take the veil, because of your childish vanity.'

He was so obtuse, so blind in his absolute faith, it was like granite in its endurance. It was incredible, she thought, that he had never suspected her lack of belief in God. It never occurred to him that she was moulded in a different cast; he gained in faith what he lacked in imagination. He believed in God as he believed in external reality, that the sun would rise each morning in the east, that he and she walked at that very moment on the Earth. Perhaps that was the reason she felt impelled to visit him, year after year. He was not a fool, yet he believed. Perhaps all these years she had been trying to draw faith from him, as one draws water from a well. If so, she had scarcely drawn enough to assuage her thirst. This was indeed the one matter she concealed from him, would always conceal from him.

'Never mind, Father,' she responded lightly. 'After all, and perhaps because of what I have told you of my dislike of the bedchamber, you are my favourite man.' She tucked her arm in his and continued playfully, like a child reciting a creed, 'You are a priest and naturally austere. I, too, am cold. We are well suited, are we not? Sometimes I feel as if we are one person divided in two. It is to see myself that I come so far year after year. How can I live without my other self?'

He had answered prosaically, 'You come to see me and to show the child to his grandmother and his maternal relations.'

'Very well, Father, if you will have it so. I have told you I have difficulty in feeling affection for the child. I will not pretend otherwise. He grows coarse and vulgar, like his father. But if you will have it that I am obeying what you are pleased to call my 'natural instincts,' so be it. I know I come only to see you.'

That had been some years ago. Since she had retired from active life as a courtesan, their relations had changed, had mellowed. She sought his approval of her writing. Last year she had sent Father Michel a copy of her first play, reminding him that it was he who had first told her of the conditions of the people in slavery in the colonies. She had written and re-written the play several times, first calling it *Zamore and Mirza*, and later, *L'Esclavage des Negres*. He had replied as follows:

Pont d'Herault,
May, 1788

My chere Marie,
Never will you cease to amaze me, though we have been friends for so many years. This attack of yours on slavery is badly written. The spelling alone is such that I am ashamed to have been your tutor in literacy! The play is overly sentimental. I ask of you, how likely is it that a slave will rescue a white couple after a shipwreck, and then, in gratitude, the white woman will petition her father, the slave master, to free her rescuer in particular and slaves in general? It borders on the absurd! I fear, my dear, it will not be a success. Apart from its faults as a piece of writing, it will very much offend the colonial lobby. And yet you show great humanity in your writing, more feeling for your fellows in adversity than I would ever be able to express. But take care. Marie. This is dangerous. It is audacious and foolhardy in the days in which we live. God Bless you for your passion, but be careful, I pray you.
Yours, in God,
Father Michel Dupre

Marie had smiled at the criticisms, which she acknowledged to be true, and utterly ignored the warnings. The play was a failure, as Father Michel predicted. But Marie was undeterred. The following month, while driving in the Bois de Boulogne she had seen a rabbit caught in a trap. Her attention had first been attracted by a shrill cry. Ordering the driver to stop, so she could climb down and investigate further, she saw the animal caught fast by the hind leg, pulling vainly. She stared, transfixed. It did not cry again for another half hour but continued pulling, its eyes staring out of its head in terror, the iron teeth of the trap gripping more deeply and lacerating the flesh from the leg with each tug. All the while Marie stood helplessly, for there was no possibility of freeing the tiny creature. She knew what she must do. Choking back the sickness in her throat she fetched a large stone and, with eyes screwed tight shut, she struck the rabbit hard on the back of the neck, in the manner she had seen the butcher in Montauban killing chickens when she was a child. The rabbit lay dead as the stone itself. She ran back to the carriage and ordered the driver to return immediately to the Rue de Rivoli. Once at home she flung off her bonnet and straight away sat down at her desk to scrawl her heartfelt condemnation of the use of such steel traps. When the bills were completed she took them herself and pasted them throughout the city streets. They were totally ignored.

    Marie though of these past literary failures as she took up her pen to write. She had been amazed, and bitterly disappointed, that no one seemed to care for the causes she cared for so passionately. Now, however, it would be different. They would listen now, when at last the ferment of revolutionary ideals had gripped Paris. The time had come for women to make their voices heard. Had not the common people of Les Halles brought the king himself to Paris?

'Be quiet,' she called to the great dog, *Voltaire*, gnawing a bone at her feet, and to the lovebirds, shrilling their morning song. 'I am going to write... *how* I am going to write!' She was a neophyte in her zeal and her first instinct was to write to Father Michel.

Paris,
October, 1789

Dear Father Michel,
I write to share my joy with you, that at last this day has dawned, when the banners of Liberty, Equality and Fraternity are rising in this city. The old order is falling and a better world is about to arise from the ashes of corruption and greed. I give thanks to God for the times in which we live.
With heartfelt love and thanks,
Marie.

For several hours after completing this short impassioned letter to the priest, Marie's pen scratched rapidly across the surface of her papers; she cared little for spelling, or even for coherence. What she craved was to find the words which would express the appalling realities of injustice. With the coming of the Declaration of the Rights of Man, the time was ripe for a series of socially inspired pamphlets. But where should one start, with such a morass of injustice to attack? Her thoughts went first to the plight of bastards, people like herself who belonged to no one, who were cut off from the protection of the family, cut off like branches snapped from the family tree. There should be birthright for bastards, and so she wrote with passion, interspersing the logic of her arguments with inconsequential details from her own life and her encounters with her father, the marquis. Then she wrote of the outrage of childbirth. Women lay in maternity hospitals in Paris, with no privacy whatsoever, rent by the pains of childbirth, their gaping bodies exposed to the eyes of curious onlookers. These conditions must and should be remedied. Then to poverty in general. Only the day before, she had halted her carriage on the way to theatre, to buy lavender from a poor beggar woman. Beside the woman stood a small child, very white and thin. He was silent and had a look of empty resignation. There was something very wrong with him, she was sure. She asked the woman, who simply shrugged and said,

'He starves, madame, like all Paris.'

Without further thought, Marie had lifted the child into her arms and pressed her purse into his hands, her tears flowing freely and splashing onto the red velvet of the pouch of money. The child had been too weak even to register surprise, although his mother had broken into garrulous thanks. Marie could not believe that, in all Paris, she was alone in being affected by the plight of poverty. Others must feel as she did, for in the urban squalor of the capital, starving people were all too evident. Life was a ghastly travesty, the rich hurrying to theatres and salons, banquets and masques, jostled by the abject poor. How could anyone be happy, with the daily contemplation of misery? There must be a voluntary tax on wealth. It was not as unlikely or impossible as it sounded, she assured herself, as she wrote. In principle, at least the first estate had agreed to the need for equality in taxation. This must be because, like herself, they were disgusted and sickened by what they saw, the unnatural contrasts of squalor and squander in the streets every day.

She wrote steadily for three hours, pouring passion into her writing. She was tired. Her *ouevre* must wait for another day. This was to be an adaptation of the *Declaration of the Rights of Man,* for it was by no means clear that the same principles would be granted to her own sex. She would call it, *The Declaration of the Rights of Women and the Female Citizen,* and she would dedicate it to the queen. She had idolized Marie Antionette since she had first come to France as a frivolous young *dauphine*. Marie Antionette had been much maligned since she had come to France, depicted as an insatiable sexual predator, with a taste for both men and women. She had been accused of acquiring venereal disease from the Cardinal De Rohan and spreading it among leading members of the French court. None of this was true, Marie was sure, but did not she, Olympe de Gouges, know what it was to be called a whore? The king was a delightful father! As one who had never known a true father, Marie idealised the royal family and her vision for France was one of a constitutional monarchy.

The pen slipped from her fingers and she sat, still as an alabaster statue, a small smile playing on her lips, her eyes burning like candles. She dreamed of a society in which no woman should have her invidious choice, nun, degraded wife, or courtesan. She clasped her small hands together until the whites of her knuckles showed. In her ideal society people would care to right the wrongs done to others and brotherhood and sisterhood would lock humanity together. Then they would know God at last, the God of goodness not the God as depicted by the French church. As she slipped into a half-dream, this ideal world became a reality in her mind. It was no utopian dream she told herself. It was a prophecy of what was about to happen, for had not the principles of liberty, equality and fraternity been voiced? People had taken these principles to their hearts and so too had the Bourbon king. He and his queen had shown their compassion, by returning to Paris.

Her thoughts turned again to God, and involuntarily, she slipped to her knees and praised him more ardently than she could ever remember doing in her life before, that at last he was real for her. This revolution was revelation itself, her own, intimate Revelation. She thanked God, that she, who had cursed her woman's lot and her birth itself, should be privileged to act as his witness, that all wrongs would be righted. For the first time in her life there was a true flutter of faith within her, gentle as the wings of her love-birds on her wrist, but real nevertheless. Was this, at last, the Holy Spirit of God?

Her prayers were disturbed by the sounds of a scuffle outside her window. Rising from her knees, she hurried across the room to look out. A nobleman lay in the gutter with a dagger in his throat. He looked like a stuck pig. A young man, dressed in the working clothes of a Parisian refuse worker, loped off down the street. The blood spurted from the nobleman's artery, he looked faintly ridiculous with his thin, weasel face and his pink satin-clad legs spread-eagled in the street. Marie clutched her own throat, horrified, as she had been since childhood, by the sight of blood. Such things often happened, of course. She told herself, resolutely, how common it was for street brawls to end in this way. It was unusual, perhaps, that one of the nobility should be the victim but that was the chance result of violence, nothing more. It had nothing to do with the revolution.

1790 - The Church and the Revolution

The self-styled National Assembly of France was in acute difficulties, all France was bankrupt. Where better to turn for a remedy in this crisis than to the Church of France, immensely wealthy and making only voluntary contributions, the *don gratuit,* to the exchequer? The deputies of the National Assembly turned their eyes towards the lands of the Church of France, to provide the means of survival in these uncertain times. From August 1789, deputies had begun to assert that all ecclesiastical property belonged to the nation of free citizens. After all, why not? Was it right that those who claimed to be the followers of the poor Nazarene carpenter should grow fat, should gorge themselves on the fruits of the pastures of France? How was this compatible with liberty, equality and the brotherhood of man? Of course, these strictures applied only to the higher clergy, the bishops and archbishops. All of them were noblemen. The poor clergy lived as wretchedly as the peasants whose souls they tended. Their lot could be improved.

So said Talleyrand, the radical and ambitious Bishop of Autun. The sale of church lands would supply two milliards of livres. If the state were to take over the financial responsibilities of the church, even while committing to paying an annual salary of not less than 1,200 livres to the poorer parish priests, everyone would benefit and the financial crisis would be averted. It was a simple solution and a good one, said Talleyrand. He was a far-sighted man, though no favourite of the king, who preferred his bishops to believe in God. Belief in God had little or no part in Talleyrand's thinking. The future, as far as Talleyrand could see, might easily bring about the collapse of the decayed and creaking edifice of the French Church. Better to creep from the building while the plaster was only cracked, before the plaster came caving in over one's head. He proposed not only the sale of church lands but the abolition of plurality of office, amazing for one so much blessed with sinecures. There was to be a new method of appointment to ecclesiastical office. All active citizens with voting rights were to be allowed to elect bishops and priests. The new organization was to follow the democratic principles enshrined in the Declaration of Rights. Again, why not, since this was the New Age of liberty, equality and freedom? The influence of Voltaire and the *philosophes* began to be felt in France. In practice this could mean a clergyman might be appointed by a group of men consisting of Protestants, Jews, infidels, not a single Catholic! This was a far cry from the movement towards self-government proposed by Richer.

But this imposition of a Civil Constitution on the mighty edifice of the church by a high-handed secular National Assembly had absolutely no precedent. Religious schism was inevitable. The clergy were to be required to swear an oath of loyalty to the Civil Constitution. They simply did not know what to do. Should their loyalty be to France and the revolution or to the pope in Rome? After months of delay the king, prevaricating as usual, brought himself to a decision and ratified the Civil Constitution. The sanction of Pope Pius VI was sought in the autumn of 1790. But no word came from the pope. The French clergy, divided and hesitant, awaited a lead from him but the pope followed the example of the French king and delayed his decision. He was anxious not to imperil the papal possessions of Avignon and the Venaissin. The deputies of the National Assembly knew that Pius VI had no love for the revolution, but Rome usually capitulated in the end. How slow, though were the cogs of the wheels of the antiquated laws of Rome! December came. In less than four weeks, all French priests were to be required to swear the oath of loyalty to the Civil Constitution publicly, in their towns and villages after Sunday Mass. And still no word from that crusty old fool, Pius VI, thought the reformers! For them the delay was maddening. For the priests of France it was a time of acute anxiety, to swear or not to swear?

Father Michel of Pont d'Herault was sitting in the cottage of his fellow priest, Father Pierre Bastain, this dark December night. He held out his hands to the cheering wood fire, as Father Pierre bustled about the tiny room, burrowing like a fat stoat into a wooden closet to bring out the better than usual *vin rouge* in his guest's honour. These meetings between the priests were rare, for twelve kilometres separated their villages, and there was only an ancient mule for transport. Aside from their common priesthood, it was difficult to see what held them together in friendship. Father Bastain was a round cottage-loaf of a man, with a red face and eyes like currants. He had once had ambitions to rise from the obscurity of parish priest in a remote Languedoc village, but he had been hampered by overfondness for the bottle, and, if rumour was true, for his female parishioners, in his younger days. Not that celibacy was an insurmountable obstacle, for the French clergy. One had to be discreet, of course. He had often wondered about the relations between his brother priest and the beautiful woman who visited him year after year, for love of him, many said. But he had never dared to ask Father Michel. He looked at him now as he poured wine into two earthenware goblets. Father Michel's profile was emaciated and hawk-like in the candlelight. His cavernous eyes were fixed dreamily on the flames of the fire. There was something austere and remote about him. Father Bastain would never dare to ask him about his relations with women.

Besides, there were more important affairs they needed to discuss. Though they were far from Paris and the feverish activity of revolutionary politics, this business of the oath to the Civil Constitution was something that concerned them all. He must consult with his brother priest, for there was a certain integrity about Father Michel which commanded respect. He was not a comfortable companion, but he was a fervent man of God. Father Pierre hitched up his cassock and plumped himself down in a chair on the other side of the fire, offering a goblet of wine to Father Michel.

'Well, brother,' he began. 'What of this oath for all the clergy? Will you swear?'

Father Michel turned his face towards his friend. His eyes seemed to take a while to focus, as if he was returning from thoughts of some far distant place. At length he replied,

'I confess I should like to. There is much that is good in the reforms that the new government propose, I believe. It would be good for the welfare of the people, that they should take more responsibility. There are measures which would encourage them to become more involved in affairs.'

Father Pierre waved aside the people and their involvement in affairs.

'Never mind the people! What matters is that our stipends are to be increased, Father. And not before time, say I. Why, the difference in the incomes of the higher clergy and we poor parish priests, it's scandalous!'

Father Michel shrugged indifferently, then replied,

'That may be so. However, Father Pierre, I fear it will not be possible to swear. No sanction has reached France, from the pope. The time grows short, too short, I believe, for His Holiness' reply to reach us here in France, before the day appointed for the swearing of the oath.' He smiled serenely. 'So there is an end to the matter.'

'An end!' spluttered his friend. 'I think not, indeed! That old fool, Pius V1, he has his own reasons for keeping us on the edge of our chairs, I doubt not.'

'What can you possibly mean, Father? What reasons could he have? There must be many more weighty matters to occupy His Holiness. That would account for the delay.' He paused and added, sadly,

'I would beg of you, my friend, not to speak irreverently of the Holy Father. It pains me that you, a brother priest, should do so.'

'Pah... you are too generous, too naive, my friend.' He eyed his fellow priest narrowly. But there could be no doubt of the sincerity in that ascetic face. 'Do you not know, my friend, what delays the pope? All Christendom knows that the papal states in Avignon are in revolt, and that the pope needs the help of the deputies of the new National Assembly to put down the rising. Were it not for that, he would condemn the Declaration of Rights, the oath for the clergy and the revolution altogether. The pope has no love for the French clergy, brother, he but waits to see which way the wind will blow!'

'That I do not believe!' said Father Michel crisply.

The other shook his head.

'Popes are politicians, Father Michel. Perhaps they have to be. But as surely as Christ died on the cross, Pius is politician first, priest second.'

'He is my brother in Christ, as you are, my friend. But above all, he is the successor of Peter. I shall abide by his ruling and I beg you to do so also.'

Father Pierre tried a different tactic;

'They say the voice of God himself speaks through the mouths of his deputies, for all the good they would bring to France.'

'That cannot be,' replied Father Michel, firmly. 'You and I know that the voice of God speaks through Pope Pius V1, the successor of Peter. He can speak through none other, for Christ himself ordained it so. That is the law of the church and thus it is the law of God. Would you have me disobey my God?'

'I would have you behave like a sensible man, Father, and take the rewards that are justly due to you,' was the earnest reply. Tears came to the eyes of the fat priest as he contemplated his friend. Did the man not realise the likely consequences, if he refused to take the oath? At the very least, he would be ousted from his parish. And that might be only the beginning of his troubles.

'I beg you to swear, Father Michel. *Il faut bien vivre,*

n'est-ce pas?'

'Assuredly, my friend, one must live until the time comes to die. But one must live with oneself, above all. I cannot swear.'

So the conversation turned in a desultory way to parish matters, the state of the stores of winter fodder, the attitudes of stubborn peasants towards their priests, the jealousy they showed because of their priests' alleged influence over their women in the confessional. Before long, Father Michel rose to depart. He had a long ride home on the mule. The muffled sound from behind the sacking curtains indicated the first snowflakes had begun to fall. As he hunched his shoulders into his cloak at the door Father Pierre said,

'You will reconsider, Father?'

'My mind is firm, I believe.'

The other priest shook his head sadly and added,

'If you are displaced, as you will be, if a constitutional priest is appointed in your stead, you can always seek refuge here.'

'I thank you. It is written, *the Son of Man has nowhere to lay his head.* But yours is a kind offer and I shall not forget it.'

Father Pierre withdrew, puzzled. Father Michel was not 'the Son of Man,' good priest though he was. The man was perhaps a little unbalanced, fanatical in his faith. He feared greatly for his future.

But Father Michel rode home slowly and serenely, gazing at the dark outlines of the trees, their branches stretched against the night sky like Satan's fingers. The mule's hooves were muffled by the snow which fell continuously and covered the land with a virgin blanket. So must the first Christmas have been like this night, he mused, never considering that Palestine could never have experienced this season, this covering of virgin snow. Things were as he perceived them. There was never another perspective for the priest.

Four weeks later, the snow had fallen heavily over the Languedoc countryside, and lay like a blanket over the village of Pont d'Herault. It muffled the footsteps of the procession of parishioners who were wending their way up the hill to the church of Mary Queen of Sorrows this bitterly cold morning. Up the hill they trailed, their heads bent low against the stinging snowflakes. From where Father Michel stood, from the vantage point of the crest of the hill, they looked like an army of black beetles, marching inexorably forward. His breath condensed on the frosty air and he smiled sardonically. There were many more parishioners than might have been expected in this inclement weather, and one would have to be a fool not to know the reason why. Not for love of the Mass, assuredly, and not for love of him. His austere, finicky ways alienated him from the village folk. He lacked the common touch, he knew, and was beloved by very few. Undoubtedly this great turnout was due to the fact that this was the day ordained by the National Assembly for all the clergy of France to swear the oath to the new constitution. They came, not to experience again the mystery of Christ made flesh on the altar, but to hear what he would have to say afterwards. He was extraordinarily indifferent to this fact. As always he was absorbed in the ecstasy of anticipation, that his was the privilege of summoning God to the altar.

He turned into the church to assure himself that all was prepared for the Mass. He smoothed an imaginary crease in the altar cloth before entering the sacristy to be ritually garbed by a red-nosed altar boy, snivelling from the cold. As he moved between the sacristy and the altar, he was only vaguely aware of the peasants filing in, banging the snow from their boots in the porch and blowing their frost-nipped fingers to warm them. A few of them, with sighs and the creaking of arthritic joints, forced themselves clumsily to their knees, to ask forgiveness for their sins, before the Mass began. Most did not. Those kneeling were distracted in their petitions by the jostling and pushing as yet more people were arriving to find their places in the house of God. The tiny church was packed. No one noticed the sound of the wheels of a chaise stopping outside, or the entry of a heavily veiled woman who took her place silently at the back of the church.

The timeless word of the Mass were repeated by Father Michel, each time was, for him, a new spiritual orgasm. He completed the Mass and cleaned the sacred vessels slowly and methodically before turning to face the congregation. Then he spoke.

'It is most gratifying that so many of you are here present in church this morning. I believe it is because of the oath I am required to make today to the new constitution of France. And yet you all know what I must say. His Holiness, Pope Pius V1 has not seen fit to sanction the changes to the status of the Church of France which our National Assembly would impose. Therefore it is impossible for me to say the words you have no doubt come to hear me say. I say instead this: I swear an oath of loyalty to His Holiness the Pope in Rome. He is the Holy Father of our church. His is the voice of God. To him I swear my oath.'

His voice rang out coldly and clearly and he placed his long white hands on the Bible as he spoke. He looked at no one, but out beyond the closed doors of the church porch as if speaking to the world beyond this simple congregation. Then his voice warmed and the focus of his gaze receded and ranged over each individual seated below the pulpit as he said,

'As your pastor, I warmly recommend you to continue to come as you have so conscientiously today, to receive the blessed sacrament at my hands. You could do nothing better, for the salvation of your souls.'

He did not bless them again but turned and walked purposefully into the sacristy. The peasants trudged out silently. In the church porch they began to mutter and their mutterings became a rumbling as they descended through the drifting snow to the village of Pont d'Herault.

The woman at the back of the church sat motionless until the congregation had departed. Then, with a sudden gesture, she threw back her veiling, revealing her light coloured hair. She rose and walked quickly down the narrow aisle and entered the sacristy without knocking, startling Father Michel in the act of pulling the vestments over his head. She faced him.

'Marie! he cried. 'I was not expecting you here!'

'Not expecting me?' she replied bitterly. 'Not expecting me? I would not for the world have stayed away on the day I was expecting so much from *you!* I came through the winter snow, through days of uncomfortable travel, to hear the voice of the man I have admired so much in my life, give assent to the cause I so much cherish.' Her voice had grown shrill but she added, on a lower note, 'I have been cruelly disappointed.'

'I could do nothing else,' he protested. 'You know, as I do, that the pope has not sanctioned these changes.'

'The pope!' she retorted. 'Who is the pope? Do you tell me he speaks for God, for Christ, who succoured the poor?'

'I do,' he replied, simply.

'Then you are a fool!' she cried. 'And I never thought to speak so to a priest, to a man I have respected since I was a child. Do you not concede that these changes brought about by the revolution will benefit the people, will alleviate their burden of poverty and taxation?'

'As a man, I do. I only hope the people will prove capable of realising their benefits. In time, perhaps, the pope will see fit to sanction the Civil Constitution of France. My hope is that he will do so. For the present, since he has not, I am bound by my oath of obedience to my church. This first and great oath must take precedence over the one you would have me swear today. Marie, cannot you see this?'

'I cannot,' she replied stonily. 'No matter. My allegiance is now elsewhere. I have revered and respected you, but there is now another man who commands my loyalty.'

Father Michel's eyes narrowed and his anger matched her own as he spoke,

'I see, Marie. You have a new lover, I suppose?'

She stamped her foot. Her dewy, harebell eyes turned to granite. Was this the effect she had intended? Did she know herself whether she meant to deceive him, to taunt him? She did not know herself whether she was playing a part, but her outrage seemed genuine as she retorted,

'Shame that you should assume so! I told you, several years ago, that is all over. I had thought our hearts beat as one, that we shared the same hopes. Even that our souls were like two halves of a broken shell that could be locked together and no one should see where they joined. To come all this way to hear your treachery... when I came to hear you echoing my dearest sentiments, as I believed you must!' Her voice rose shrilly, dramatically.

'But Marie, I simply do not understand you!' he cried helplessly. 'I am sorry to disappoint you. But who do you mean? To whom have you given your loyalty?'

She pressed her lips together in mulish silence. She would prolong his uncertainty.

'Please tell me, dear,' he continued humbly. His lip trembled. 'As for the oath, I tell you again I am sorry to disappoint you. But I can do nothing else. I have no choice.' His voice rose to a pitch to match her own. 'I have no choice but to choose my church before anything else!'

'And I choose my king before anyone else,' she murmured, quiet at last.

'The king?' he echoed stupidly.

'Yes,' she replied. 'I pledge my allegiance to Louis XV1, Louis Capet, as he will soon simply be called.' She continued, in a dreamy voice, 'He is a good husband. A good father, too. Something I have never had.'

He looked at her incredulously. How was it possible for a woman of her experience and intelligence to be so simple-minded?

'Do not be a fool, Marie! Is it possible you do not understand that Louis Capet, as you imagine he will happily style himself, is a coward and a weakling? He appears at the moment to support the revolution, yes, because he has no choice. He is virtually a prisoner of the National Assembly. You, who have lived in the centre of politics in Paris, must know this as well as I.'

'I know nothing of the kind,' she retorted. 'The king has pledged his support for the Revolution, which means support for the people. And he, Father, has much more to lose than you!'

'Indeed, he has all of France to lose,' he replied sardonically. 'He has so much to lose that it is my belief he will yet make an attempt to retain it. He will betray the revolution, if it is at all possible for him to do so.' He strode to the end of the sacristy, then returned to her and, taking her shoulders into his hands, looked deeply into her eyes. 'But you are wrong to say he has more to lose than I, Marie. He has France, yes, but I have my God.'

'No one asks you to disobey your God, she replied. 'You are asked merely to disobey the institution of the church, and that pious prig, the pope. It is not at all the same thing.'

'For me it is,' he declared, simply. 'I would betray my calling to the priesthood.'

'No one, not even I, Father Michel, have ever asked you to betray your calling.' She murmured the words gently, and her eyelids dropped. His fingertips clutched her shoulders, at these words, and, impetuously, he clasped her to his breast, as her meaning penetrated his mind. He felt a sudden stirring in his loins as he embraced her, but the seed of deception in his mind told him it was an instinct of protection. This woman he cared for deeply seemed resolved on a path of dangerous impetuosity. Yet he held her, held her as if he could never let her go. Many silent minutes passed between. At last he released her.

'Marie, I beg of you, do not make public your support for the king. You are becoming well-known in the capital through your radical literature. That is good, you think?'

'You flatter me,' she responded, simpering a little.

'Far from flattering, I would warn you!' he retorted. 'What you are doing is dangerous, will be dangerous if the tide of politics turns against the king.'

'I speak not of politics, but of principles, Father. I, too, choose to follow my calling, to act on principle where the Revolution is concerned.'

'Your love for the revolution is fanatical!' he cried.

'As is yours for the church. As I have told you before, Father, we are alike. We two are carved from the one stone.'

'I do not understand you at all!' he cried, impatiently.

'You deceive yourself. You choose not to understand me or to understand yourself. The stones we are carved from might well be flung to the far corners of the earth, since they cannot lie together. *Au Revoir,* Father Michel.'

She turned and, without a backward glance, walked quickly to the door of the church and up the steps to the waiting carriage.

1791 Marie writes for the Women of France

Honorine was in the kitchens of the apartment in the Rue de Rivoli, where the cook-maid was chopping parsley and carrots for the midday soup. It was a sweltering day in June, 1791, and the darkness of the kitchen was penetrated by shafts of sunlight which heightened the intensity of heat from the stove, where the soup pot was bubbling. The young cook-maid turned from her task and, wiping her hands on her apron, looked enquiringly at the older maidservant.

'Annette, I think you should prepare a little salad for m'lady's luncheon today. Some sorrel and cheese, perhaps, and some soft white bread rolls, if they can be procured. In this heat, I fear she will not drink soup.'

'No,' agreed the younger maid. 'I will do as you ask, Honorine, though I doubt she will eat it. She eats nothing these days.'

Honorine pressed her lips together grimly.

'No, indeed, it is this accursed writing. It saps her strength, and it is scarcely natural in a woman, it seems to me. Why cannot she go about and show her beauty in the salons and assemblies, like other women of her kind?' she cried out in exasperation, forgetting that it was unseemly to criticise her mistress to the cook-maid. Remembering this, she paused and spoke in more distant tones.

'Nevertheless, you will do as I ask, Annette. And please

change your apron before you take the food to your mistress. You know she cannot abide dirt, it will take away what appetite she has. Although, in this household of animals, it takes me all my time to remove the grime!' She reverted again to the role of *confidante,* for in truth, though she was a loyal servant, the behaviour of her mistress worried her greatly.

The food was brought to Marie as she sat at her writing desk. She paused long enough to bestow a gracious smile on the serving girl, but ate little. The airless room was quiet again as the girl crept silently away. All that could be heard was the scratching of Marie's quill, and the occasional grunt of the Great Dane, *Voltaire,* who lay slumped at her feet. She passed a hand through her hair, the curling tendrils were sticking to her cheeks in the heat. Her face was pale, though the translucence of her skin, through prolonged fasting, added to her beauty. From time to time, she brushed away a tear, as she poured her passionate feelings into her writing. The pamphlet was entitled, *Declaration of the The Rights of Woman and the Female Citizen,* and it was to be her most important, the one she had been planning to write before she had been distracted by the matter of the clerical vote. Too much time had been wasted in fruitless and frustrating travel to visit Father Michel, who would not, or could not see the sense of the Civil Constitution. Now she must concentrate. She opened with an embittered inquiry; why, she asked, had men chosen to subjugate women?

Oh man, are you capable of justice? By what sovereign right do you oppress my sex? It is a woman who poses the question; you will not deprive her of that right at least.

This heartfelt cry was followed by a host of personal

details. She wrote of her own enforced marriage to Louis Aubry, her only choice, other than the living death of the cloister. She wrote of the horrors of childbirth and, inconsequentially, of the iniquities of a cab driver who had overcharged her while she was going about the city, distributing her pamphlet supporting the king as constitutional monarch. Most of her arguments were lucid and penetrating, but hers was a skittish intelligence, she darted from one matter to another like a butterfly sipping nectar from flowers. She knew her powers of thinking were as great, or greater, then those of countless male citizens who had been given the right to vote through the Declaration of the Rights of Man. She echoed the paragraphs of this document in her demands for women. But as she wrote, she caught sight of her face in the gilded mirror above her desk and could not resist expressing herself thus:

The sex superior in beauty as in its courage in the course of maternal suffering recognises and declares in the presence of the Supreme Being the following rights of Women and the Female Citizen. There shall be equal rights with men, before the law, in civic matters, in taxation and ownership of property. The law must be the expression of the general will. All female and male citizens must contribute either personally, or through their representatives in its formation. It must be the same for all. All female and male citizens, being equal in its eyes, must be equally admitted to all honours, positions and public employment according to their capacity and with no distinctions beyond those of their talents and virtues. No one must be disturbed for expressing their basic convictions. Woman has the right to mount the scaffold: she has equally the right to mount the rostrum.

She paused and re-read this last sentence. She liked its neatness and incisiveness, but she shuddered as her mind lingered on the truth of her statement. This was becoming a bloody revolution, there was no denying it. She, who had hated the sight of blood since childhood, shut her eyes as she remembered the haunted, fearful eyes of men and women packed like cattle in tumbrils as they were herded to the scaffold. It was sights like these, more than the dastardly behaviour of the cabman, that had chilled her when she had made her latest distributing tour of the Parisian streets. Opening her eyes, she shrugged, resolutely. This was doubtless the fault of men. Women, she felt sure, were capable of revolution without terror and violence. Why should not this be possible, in the name of reason? Thinking of the brutal aspects of the revolution increased her fervour to pour all her eloquence into the cause of women's rights.

Women, awake! The toscin of enlightenment and reason resounds through the universe. Recognise your rights!

Pausing again, and resting her slender, aching hand on her chin, she thought how little she had done, until now, to live according to these principles. She thought of the succession of men in her bed, the means by which she had amassed a fortune. The means by which she had arrived at independence was hopelessly flawed, was in many ways despicable. In that, Father Michel was right, though he had no alternative to suggest, save obscurity and the denial of her sex, through the cloister. She caught sight of herself in the mirror, and coquettishly, twitched the lace at her throat. She was still beautiful, she knew. Only recently she had had a letter from her friend and helpmate, Mirabeau, turned adviser to the king. He had written,

Until now I had thought the graces adorned themselves only with flowers, but your thoughts are expressed with fluency and power. You are the flower of the revolution.

She cherished the words, for Mirabeau was an old friend, he had advised and helped her when she first came to Paris. He had always been ugly, though charming, but now he was dead. She had grieved for him when she heard the news two months ago. She thought of that other man, tall and straight in faraway Languedoc. He was very much alive, she knew well what that hardness had meant, when he had clasped her to himself in the sacristy of the church. But he refused to know it, because of his stubborn vows. She had lain awake many nights, since she had abandoned her trade as a courtesan, hugging to herself certain words he he once spoken. 'You are wrong about me, Marie. Since the day you told me you would marry Louis Aubry, I have known I am no natural celibate.' For him, chiefly, she had given up her profession. So she told herself. But it was not important now. The nocturnal empire of women such as she had been, was being swept away by the revolution. The time had come when women would no longer be subject to the will of men. In her youth, this had been the only means of securing wealth and independence, but this was no longer so. She, more than anyone, must face the task of letting the world know. She wrote on, resolutely.

Women have been responsible for more harm than good. Constraint and dissimulation has been their lot. What they could not gain by force they gained by ruse, using all the resources of their charms. They must claim their dues now, honestly, and end their dependence on the whims of men. This must be achieved by better education and employment opportunities.

She paused again. Once, long ago and for a short time, she had played the role of wife and mother. But she shuddered more, when she thought of marriage, than when she thought of the tumbrils clattering through the streets of Paris. For her, marriage was a vision of herself spread-eagled in a lumpy bed in a tiny, airless, odorous room in Languedoc. Herself in agony, in the valley of the shadow of death, the victim of an old man's lust. She picked up her pen.

Marriage is the tomb of love and trust. There must be a looser form of contract, and provision made for women to claim their rights to be spared the pains of successive childbirth, which is beyond human endurance.

Her memory plummeted back still further. She saw herself again as a small child, standing holding the horse of a nobleman. His lascivious eyes were upon her. He spoke to her contemptuously. Her rancour against the Marquis Lefranc de Pompignan was fresh in her mind. She wrote, vehemently.

There must be provision for the rights of natural children.

Marie had always found it easier to live in the world of her imagination than in the grim realities of existence. She mused on her ideals of marriage. It was a rarefied, affectionate state, respecting and respectable. Something perhaps, like the depictions of the Holy Family in scripture. She resolved to dedicate her pamphlet to the queen, Marie Antoinette. Though a queen, she was also a wife and mother. It was difficult to imagine the queen in childbed, she was so pretty, refined and remote, like a china doll. But it needed someone of greater influence than herself, Olympe de Gouges, to further women's rights, and who better than the former queen who had declared she would relinquish her hereditary rights?

I dedicate this paper to Marie Antoinette, erstwhile Queen of France and queen of my sex. She, with her adored husband, Louis Capet, has made the greatest possible sacrifice for France, giving up her title for the good of the revolution and the welfare of the people.

She sighed when she thought about the king. Actually, thinking about him was difficult, for she had never actually seen him. But because this was so, it was easier to fantasize about him. People said he was tall, kindly looking, some said rather simple minded, obsessive as he was about his hobby, the art of the locksmith. It was rumoured that in the early days of his marriage, he had difficulty in being a true husband. Would Father Michel have had this difficulty, she wondered? Really, she must stop thinking about him, this idle musing was fruitless. Never, never could they have been man and wife, their destinies had been forged otherwise. He had been a priest since she was a small child, after all. Now, though they were ostensibly friends, they quarrelled. Partly, it was the matter of unacknowledged attraction which came between them. (Unacknowledged on his part, though, for herself, she had more insight, more experience, more honesty.) But now there was this much greater difference, this matter of the revolution. He, and priests like him, were tearing France asunder by their obstinate refusal to take the oath of loyalty to the new constitution of France. The unity of the revolution was being undermined by stubborn priests, for in April, Pope Pius V1 had finally issued a papal bull condemning the Civil Constitution.

Now Father Michel would never sign, she knew, so now their relationship must finally be severed. She would transfer her affections from one unobtainable man to another. At least the king was not a hypocrite, a man who pretended not to be a man. He was suitably remote, unknown to her and therefore a better subject for her fantasies. She must love someone, after all.

The next morning, Marie lay in bed, feverish and unwell. Her writing and perhaps, even more, her thinking, had exhausted her. She would allow no one near her, except *Voltaire* and *Rousseau*. The bed curtains were drawn and the room was dark. *A rainforest in the slave colonies must be like this*, she thought, feverishly, as the beads of perspiration glistened on her brow, for the room was pervaded by the smell of dog and monkey, and the freshly squeezed oranges brought by Honorine to tempt her mistress' palate. For two days she did not stir, then her energy returned as suddenly as it had ebbed, and she demanded Honorine should come to wash and dress her bedraggled hair and restore her neglected beauty.

'Come, Honorine, I have lost enough time. I must deliver my paper to the publisher. But first you must wash and comb me and make me fit to be seen again. While you do so, I shall read to you what I have written You will be so pleased with your mistress, *ma chere.*

She sat before the mirror and began to read. Honorine stood behind her, drying and combing her fair hair. She read with intonation and feeling, not pausing for comment, until she reached the final paragraph:

I dedicate this paper to Marie Antoinette, erstwhile Queen of France and queen of my sex. She, with her adored husband,

Louis Capet, has made the greatest possible sacrifice...

'Honorine, I beg of you, have care!' she exclaimed, feeling a sharp tug at her scalp.

'Have care, madame? It is you who must take care. You cannot publish this!'

Marie raised her eyes from the pamphlet and stared in astonishment at the woman's face in the mirror. It was deathly white, terror-stricken.

'Why, Honorine, whatever is the matter? What ails you?'

'Your recklessness, madame. You cannot, as I say, publish this. While you have been sick abed you have not heard the news which has shocked all of Paris, all of France, indeed. The king has attempted to flee the country. He has shown himself, beyond all doubt, no friend of the revolution.' She recounted her tale, slowly and contemptuously.

'Why, madame, it seems that the royal party escaped from the Tuileries in disguise. They travelled in the name of the family Von Korff. The dauphin was dressed in a girl's frock, with a wide-brimmed bonnet pulled down over his eyes. Such a sketch he must have looked! Both the royal children went, of course, and also their governess, the Duchesse de Tourzel, and their Aunt Elizabeth. And, *bien sur,* the king himself, and *Madame Deficit.* Madame, the queen was dressed as the children's governess, in a brown dress and a hat with a heavy veil, while the duchesse took the part of the children's mama. Such a come-down for her majesty to take the lower part, to have her tower of hair flattened by a governess' bonnet! Well, they travelled in a hired carriage to a *rendevous* outside the *Porte St Martin.* There they transferred to a most sumptuous berlin with dark green and yellow bodywork and yellow wheels, with white velvet upholstery inside. They must needs travel in style, in a great lumbering carriage drawn by six horses. That was their undoing, it seems. For even where the roads were good, it was impossible to drag that great, heavily laden cart at more than seven kilometres an hour. And there were accidents, I believe. A wheel struck the wall of a narrow bridge and the horses fell. They had to stop to repair the traces of the carriage. I imagine those spoiled children must have been whinging and mewing, unaccustomed as they are to any discomfort! But I am surprised you did not hear the toscin ringing, madame, when it was discovered that their apartments in the Tuileries were empty. For a great crowd surged to the palace, and people streamed inside, demanding the palace servants remove their liveries. Such a racket they made, it could be heard all over Paris.'

'I heard nothing,' replied Marie, stonily.

'Did you not madame? She continued in confidential tones, 'They say one cherry hawker got into the queen's bedchamber and sprawled herself and her wares on the quilted eiderdown.' She giggled. 'It seems she did not bother to remove her boots. She fed herself with cherries, there on the queen's bed, and she cried out, 'Now it is the turn of the nation, to be comfortable. Would that I had a man to share this bed!'

'Do not repeat these bawdy stories!' cried Marie, fiercely. 'Continue your tale, if you please.'

'They say the villagers along the whole route were aroused in their suspicions. By the unusualness of the great carriage of course, madame. And no escort of dragoons appeared, as had been promised, to protect the party. At *Pont de Somerville* the villagers had been so amazed by the unlikely appearance of a battalion of dragoons, that they feared they had come on behalf of landlords, to collect overdue rents, so they chased them into the woods, with pitchforks and muskets. Imagine, the king's brave escort chased off by a band of peasants!'

Marie said nothing, so Honorine continued.

'Well, the National Guard, under Lafayette, were summoned from Paris, and horsemen set off in all directions out of the city to halt them. It was one Captain Bayon who took the road to *Valenciennes*. And he found, on inquiring at the post-house at *Sainte Menehould,* that the young post-master, Jean Baptiste Drouet, had recognised the party. For it seemed to him that the so-called governess of the children inside the berlin was uncommonly like the queen. It seems he had seen her once. And it's true of course, that her appearance is easily called to mind, even without that tower of a hairstyle, would you not say so, madame?'

'I have never seen her,' came the distant reply from Marie.

'Have you not, m'lady? Indeed it is unlikely you will ever do so now, unless you care to view her at the scaffold. For the berlin was finally halted outside *Varennes*. And the ladies were marched into the house of a corn chandler, and made to sit on rickety chairs with the straw falling out of the seats. Imagine what a humiliation for them! And such a journey as they had, back to Paris. For they say the crowds pressed around the berlin in every village, halting its progress. The people came out of their houses to flatten their noses against the windows, to take a look at the 'Baroness Von Korff.' And they say they spat at the windows and hurled abuse at the occupants. Well, what would one expect, madame? They deserved no less.' She paused for breath and began to giggle.

'Myself, I am mystified how the queen and the aunt and the Duchess de Tourzel managed to sit through the whole journey without once getting out. For they say they sat like pokers for the whole twelve hours it took to return to Paris, never once, in their pride, asking to relieve themselves. But I heard the dauphin made water two or three times in a big silver cup, and the king himself held it for him. Can you imagine, madame?'

'I do not wish to imagine, Honorine,' replied Marie, sadly and wearily. 'I do not wish to think of it at all. Is your story complete? If so, please leave me.'

'And assuredly, you will not publish, madame?' asked Honorine, remembering at last the reason for her recital. 'It would be madness, sheer madness, to publish your pamphlet, dedicated to the queen, now it is known beyond doubt that the king and queen are the enemies of the people!'

'I will reconsider. Now, Honorine, please go.'

She called *Voltaire* and *Rousseau* to her. She stroked the dog's bony head and allowed the monkey to clamber over her shoulders, where it entwined itself around her neck like a fur collar. She did not want to think, but thoughts would intrude. The king had betrayed her. He had attempted to sneak away from Paris like a common criminal. She felt it as a personal betrayal, even though she had never met him, never even seen him. She had seen a marble statue of him and had loved that semi-divine monarch of the French. She laughed, wildly. She knew she was prone to idolatry, just as Father Michel, who had worshipped his tawdry statue of the Virgin. Men she had known carnally had worshipped her, but she had reserved her worship for those whose love she could never obtain. It was a bitter irony.

Surprised by her laughter, the dog raised his head and looked at her with his great soulful eyes. The monkey wrapped himself more closely around her neck. She thought of them, not for the first time, as the reincarnated spirits of their namesakes. They alone were trustworthy. She had thought of the revolution of an act of God, and had truly believed it would right the wrongs of the poor and bring good to the people. But God was nowhere to be found but in these blameless creatures.

1792 The September Massacres

In August 1791, Marie received a letter from Father Michel:
August, 1791
Pont d'Herault

My Dear Marie,
I write to send you my views of events which by now will be well known to you, for all of France knows, of course, of the king's attempted flight from Paris. So, the 'god' you would have worshipped has proved to be a little tarnished, has he not? I confess I am unsurprised. You will recall I warned you it would be so. I warned you to put your trust in God alone. Now I warn you to cease your support for the king, absolutely. Your name, unfortunately, is well known in Paris, and if it continues to be coupled with that of the king, you will be in grave danger. Listen I beg of you, to the friend who has ever cared for your welfare.

I confess I was disappointed in the papal bull denouncing the Civil Constitution, in April. I too, have hoped that good would come from this revolution. As for myself, I know not what will become of me. It is no longer possible for me to celebrate the Mass, the mainstay of my life. But I do not ask you to pity me, or even to think of me. You will doubtless think that my obstinacy in refusing to take the oath has brought this upon me. I pray to God, not for myself, but for the people of

France.
> But most especially, I pray for you, dear Marie. In many ways I support your concern for the rights of women. It is well that there should be opportunities for women, other than lives of degradation. Perhaps other than marriage, for I have seen through the years in this small forgotten village, how that, too, can be degrading for men and women. But I ask, you, how do you identify the cause of women with this revolution which daily becomes more brutal, is tainted with the blood of so many innocents? Answer me that, my erstwhile pupil. Answer your very affectionate,
> Tutor- in Christ.

Marie stared at the letter in her hand, then slowly screwed her fingers around it and tossed it into the fire. His letter was hectoring, offensive. She was no longer a child, and he was not her tutor. She, who had read Voltaire, and had written so eloquently for the revolution! He was right to acknowledge his obstinacy in refusing the oath, but she gave no thought to its possible consequences. She did not care where he would go or what he would do. Her loyalty was now to the king. Anger with Father Michel was necessary to preserve her fragile identity, an identity forged with the revolution. So she thought not at all about the last question in the letter.

Several days later, to her joy, the king was vindicated. He accepted the constitution. Brushing aside Honorine's cynical response, that he had no choice, since his abortive attempt to escape Paris, she added a postscript to her pamphlet.

I cannot prevent myself from stopping the press to express the pure joy which fills my heart at the news that the king has accepted the constitution. Divine providence bless him for doing so.*

Her faith in 'Divine Providence' restored, Marie set about the task of superintending the distribution of her pamphlet with customary enthusiasm. She did, however, pause to write a brief reply to Father Michel.

I beg you will no longer concern yourself with my affairs. In these momentous days of revolution we cannot agree, as we have failed to agree about so many matters in the past. My tutelage has long since ceased, and so should all correspondence between us.

Olympe de Gouges.

But her reply never found him. Father Michel was forced to leave the parish he had served so faithfully, if rather dispassionately, for so many years. His successor, a young constitutional priest, with few scruples about privacy, opened the letter and chuckled cynically over the contents. So, that was the way of it with the old bigot, who had left the house with the air of a martyr for Christ himself! The new priest was familiar with the name of one of the most notorious courtesans of all Paris. What kind of dealings had they, he wondered? Perhaps she had a *penchant* for having it under the cassock. A pity there were not more like her!

As the year progressed and a new one began, Marie became obsessed with a desire to see the king in person. In Paris, there was a resurgence of goodwill towards the monarchy, despite rumours that the king continually used his veto to block legislation towards which he was unsympathetic; he would not agree to laws to enforce the banishment and persecution of non-swearing priests. It was rumoured that he would appear in public again, at the opera. Marie determined to go, to fulfill her urge to see him in person.

'Come, Honorine, dress me in my ivory silk and find my pearls. Tonight, I must be fit to see the king!'

'There's no particular joy to be had from that,' replied the maid, without enthusiasm. 'Though indeed I am glad to see you wishing to dress and go out in public, instead of sitting at home scribbling. Why, I don't think you have moved from this apartment since the king escaped from Paris last summer, except to distribute these wretched papers of yours.'

'My writing is important, Honorine, very important for the cause of women and for the revolution itself. The power of the written word is great, though I fear it is something you do not yet understand. However, we will not speak of it now. Please make my bath ready for me. And please do not refer again to the little weakness the king showed last summer. All is forgotten, now he has accepted the constitution.'

'She is like a child about to be given a treat,' thought Honorine, indulgently, but she said no more and attended to her mistress' toilette.

Marie was so whimsical, so exacting in her demands that her appearance should be perfect, that the ballet, *Psyche,* had already begun when her carriage arrived at the opera house. She sat alone in her box, her hands clasped, half enraptured by the scene on the stage yet constantly scanning the box opposite her own, hoping there would soon be enough light to see the king and queen clearly. Suddenly the furies' dance began; they brandished their torches aloft, filling the theatre with light. She saw the faces of the king and queen, illuminated by this ghostly imitation of hell. The king was short and stout, with a flat face like a fish. His eyes were inexpressibly sad, but lifeless. In truth, he was an unattractive, troubled, dull-looking man, with a wizen-faced woman sitting beside him. Marie bit her lip and stared at them in astonishment. She felt sorry for them, she would support them, but there was no denying that the king was very different from the man she imagined in her dreams at night. She turned her head towards the stage. A sense of foreboding filled her as the furies writhed and capered and the scenes of hell were enacted before her. She was sorry she had come to the opera house.

The tide of popular support for the king was short-lived. Before the end of the year, Paris was clamouring for his execution. The stark truth was that the monarchy was redundant, there was no place for the heir of the Bourbons in the new order in France. Marie, always acutely aware of events, behaved now like a doe with its ears pricked in fear, awaiting the kill, a killing she despised in principle, for she hated the very idea of capital punishment. She confined herself again to her room, sleeping very little, eating even less and writing frenziedly. Honorine began to fear for her reason, for the ideas she poured into her reluctant maid's ears grow daily more outrageous. One day she summoned Honorine to her desk and began to read a letter she proposed to send to the president of the National Convention.

The king, I would argue, is faulty as a king, but as a man he is blameless. He is the victim of his birth, his inheritance and the unhappy advice of those sycophants who surround him. But I shall not put forward all the arguments I reserve for his defence. I ask only to be received by the convention, for it is said that only Malesherbes, an old man of nearly eighty years, has been given the task of defending the king. This difficult task is worthy of a younger age, regardless that it be proposed by one of the so-called weaker sex. I propose to help in the defence of Louis Capet, for justice and mercy require that, instead of execution, he should be given an honourable exile. Never let it be forgotten that the English heaped blame on themselves when they executed Charles I. I will plead his cause for the honour of France.

Heedless of her maid's tearful protests, Marie posted her letter on September 2nd, 1792. She then continued through the streets distributing pamphlets which urged the exile, rather than the death of the king, stoically oblivious of the insults of those of the mob who bothered to read her paper, and stepping into the gutter to retrieve those thrown carelessly aside. A tightly cloaked, wraith-like figure, she darted from street to street by lamplight, until she came to the *Rue de Seine*. The streets were strangely crowded that night. In the *Rue de Seine* she noticed a bright light in the sky and heard a great clamour of voices and clashing of steel, seeming to come from the *Rue Sainte-Marguerite*. She approached a group of women and asked them what all the commotion was about.

'madame,' answered a burly washerwoman. 'Can it be that you do not know what is happening? They're simply getting rid of the goods in the prison. And we will all be better off, I doubt not, without the Roman scum.' She laughed and clapped her hand on Marie's shoulder in a gesture of sisterhood.

'What do you mean, woman? asked Marie, bewildered and appalled.

'They're butchering the priests, I mean.' The woman

shouted in her ear, for indeed it was necessary to do so to make herself heard above the screams of the victims. 'Look, look there in the gutter.'

Marie stared down. The gutter ran with blood. From inside the prison walls the screams rose to a crescendo. Marie closed her eyes in horror and clapped her hands to her ears. Her head spun as she saw again the eyes of the pigs when the butcher at Montauban was sticking them, so many years ago. She heard again their gurgling cries. Opening her eyes she saw, by the light of the bonfire which the executioners had lit to illuminate their deeds, that now they were dragging out the prisoners. They were mostly elderly priests, and, judging from their habits, of the lower orders of the clergy.

'But they are *priests*!' she cried in anguish, to anyone who would listen.

'Mais, oui,' replied the washer-woman patiently. 'Have I not said so?' Was this strange woman who questioned her perhaps half-witted? 'And a just fate for them too, say I. Why, they would treat us so, if they could come into our houses and find we had thrown out all the holy pictures!'

'They would not, indeed they *would not* act with such barbarism!' cried Marie, thinking of that tall, dark man with the Christ-like profile. 'How could you think so?'

'Look what's happening!' replied her companion, giggling inanely and ignoring Marie's outburst.

Marie looked. The priests were gesticulating wildly and shrieking to each other. The subject of their discourse seemed, appallingly, to be the best way to die quickly, to avoid the greatest pain. For they had seen, with senses heightened by acute fear, that those of their companions who raised their hands to avoid the blows of the cudgels, suffered the longest. There was no dignity in their dying, and none in the immediate aftermath. For the priests were stripped naked by their executioners and their habits taken as perquisites. The naked bodies were piled into carts. The carts were filled with naked bodies whose limbs were still flexible because there had been no time for them to grow cold. Heads and arms lay entwined together like a mass of grisly octopuses. Women helped to load the bodies into the carts and from time to time stopped to dance the *Carmagnole*. Sometimes they danced on bodies actually lying in the gutter, and laughed uproariously as their steps were hindered by the slipperiness of the bloody bodies. They fell drunkenly into the street beside the dead. One woman, finding herself lying so, grasped a naked corpse in a voluptuous embrace and tried to haul him to his feet, that he too might dance the revolutionary dance. They fell together, the quick and the dead, in a horrible embrace.

Marie could endure no more. Hurrying home to the *Rue de Rivoli,* blinded by tears, she arrived at last, so white and shocked that her teeth rattled in her head and her breath came in great gasps. Honorine chaffed her hands and spoke to her soothingly, but one thing only occupied her mind. A carriage must be ordered immediately to take her to Languedoc. It was only with extreme difficulty that Honorine managed to help her to her bed, as she persuaded her to wait until the morning.

1792 Meeting in Pont d'Herault

It was a humid day of sunless heat. The sky was an oppressive grey glare. There was no wind and the flies buzzed in swarms around the horses' heads as the carriage bumped and jolted along the rutted roads towards Languedoc. Marie was anxious to reach her destination in the shortest possible time, so she spared no expense, changing horses frequently and commanding the driver to make speed as fast as possible, from one dreary inn to the next. Even though the horses were driven as fast as her compassion for the beasts would allow, the progress was painfully slow and uncomfortable. Each night in the poky, dirty inns, she tossed feverishly, barely snatching more than two or three hours' sleep and endlessly rehearsing what she would say to Father Michel. She reflected not at all on the fact that she had not written to him for a year, and that her last letter had been one of fractious impatience with his intransigence.

As the carriage jerked and swayed she clutched the tasselled hangings and peered out of the window. Peasants, toiling over the harvest, seemed dirtier, more haunted in their expressions than she remembered on previous journeys. The carriage bowled along and, glancing out of the window she saw a group of women, their posteriors raised towards the grey blankness of the sky as they toiled. They straightened themselves as they heard the clatter of approaching hooves and glared malevolently at the carriage, shaking their fists and shouting crude oaths, their eyes glaring from their sockets.

'The people grow bolder,' thought Marie. 'The revolution has given them assurance. But it has brutalized them.' She was well aware that they mistook her for an aristocrat, for very few carriages such as the one she had hired passed through the provinces of France these days. She had never been afraid of the people; she was one of them.

'It is I, Olympe de Gouges!' she cried through the window. 'You do not know me, but I am a friend of the people. I write for the women of the revolution!'

Her voice caught on the wind. It faded into nothingness and went unheard by the women, who had resumed their work and had once again bent to the golden stubble beneath their feet.

Inside the carriage, Marie rehearsed obsessively the arguments she would employ when she finally reached Father Michel. The first essential was that he would agree to leave France. The massacre she had witnessed convinced her of the need to leave immediately. The danger was acute. Many priests had become emigres; no part of France, however remote, was a safe hiding place for a priest. This was the conviction which had brought her on this journey. He must be warned. It might well be that he was aware of the danger, that he would have gone sooner, but for lack of money. There she would be able to help him, for it had been her sole ambition to achieve independence during her life as a courtesan and she had succeeded admirably. Now was the time to share her riches. Her work in France was nearly completed; she would defend the king and then, her writing published and the revolution accomplished, she would leave France with Father Michel.

In her reverie, she thought of other arguments she would use in persuading Father Michel. In Paris, the idea of the Supreme Being was being circulated, fruit of the great minds of the Enlightenment. *God* was merely a word, a human word construct, trying to explain some Ultimate Reality beyond the powers of human explanation but known to the experiential core of men and women. *God* was a god beyond and above the church, known to innate human consciousness and affirmed by reason. *God* was not to be found in ritual formulas and symbolic bits of flattened bread. She had known this as a child, since the failure of her first communion at the age of seven. It was affirmed by the philosophy which had informed her education and now by the people, who rejected the church. For hundreds of years the church had been intrinsically associated with the monarchy, now to be rejected for its corruption and depravity. Christianity could not be rescued from the debacle. It was impossible to sever one decaying institution without destroying the other; both must go and the entrails of the church would spill forth when the limbs of the monarchy were lopped off. Of course, she would fight for the life of the king, on humanitarian grounds. But the former priests of France would have new lives open to them. Everywhere, they were renouncing their vows, emigrating, marrying, becoming the men God intended them to be. One of them should be Father Michel. She imagined what she would say to him.

'A new Spirit is being born. Purged by flames of fire, the Supreme Being is born. In the general conflagration of plaster virgins and twisted crucifixes, the Spirit of Reason comes into being. The festivals will no longer be celebrations of St Peter and St Paul and all the motley collection of eccentrics and masochists. They will be celebrations of innate God-Consciousness, Festivals of Reason!'

Marie's imagination was fired by what she believed to be the truth of her words. Her excitement was fanned and her conviction grew as she rehearsed the words she would say. She never paused to consider how Father Michel might reply. Gradually her thinking drifted into a dream of euphoric peace and emptiness, as each mile brought her further to her journey's end. She became oblivious of the jolting of the carriage along the rutted roads and the malevolent faces of the peasants as they passed through the villages of France. Six days passed before the carriage reached the village of Pont d'Herault, but for Marie the weariness was eclipsed by the joy of her musings. The last days passed in a blessed daydream of an unimaginable future for herself and Father Michel. The blessedness lay in the impossibility of really knowing what it would be like. It was like a childhood hope of Heaven, celestial and indeterminate.

As the end of the journey approached, her senses were revived by memories. She knew so well every milestone, every turn in the road, every poor, misshapen cottage and these realities thrust themselves upon her. Nothing had changed, nothing at all. She twisted her fingers in excitement as the carriage approached the church, her voice unnaturally high as she directed the driver where to stop. Then she gathered up her skirts and ran to the door of Father Michel's cottage, not stopping to knock but flinging herself across the threshold in joyous anticipation of the reunion she had rehearsed every day since she left Paris.

'*Bonjour madame.* To what do I owe this pleasure?'

She heard the surprised, sardonic greeting before she actually saw the young constitutional priest who was Father Michel's replacement. He was a young, red-haired young man, fresh-faced but with a lewd, unpleasant smile.

'I beg your pardon,' stammered Marie, in complete confusion. 'I had thought to find Father Michel Dupre here. He has lived here for many years.'

'But no longer, I fear,' replied her host. 'I am now the incumbent of this so delightfully obscure parish. To whom have I the honour of addressing?'

'My name is Olympe de Gouges,' said Marie, abstractedly, hardly taking in what he was saying, so grave was her disappointment. Then she aroused herself and said more urgently, 'I pray you tell me where Father Michel is gone?'

'Ah, the friend from Paris!' exclaimed the young man. 'I congratulate you on the tenacity of your friendship, madame. To come all this way to enjoy the company of your old friend. Such touching devotion!' He grinned, meaningfully. Marie, though fully aware of his intimations, could scarcely trouble herself to dispel them.

'Please tell me where I can find Father Michel.'

'Your name is known to me, madame,' continued the young man, still ignoring her question. 'Allow me to introduce myself. I am Andre Gaudin, happily at your service. Happy to act as a substitute for Father Michel, in the priesthood... and in other ways.'

'Cease your detestable insinuations!' replied Marie, roused to anger at last. 'Where is Father Michel?'

'We do not call him *Father*, you understand,' replied F.Gaudin, still maddeningly evading her question. 'We who support the revolution do not recognise those who have refused to give their oath to the constitution of France. You, madame, as a supporter of the new order in France will naturally understand this.' He paused and smiled again, a lascivious gleam in his eye.

'I wonder, madame, that you do not think to turn your favours to one who has so much more in common with you. In politics and in pleasure.'

'Please answer my question.' Marie stamped her foot. 'I have not come all this way to bandy words with one such as you!'

'Michel Dupre is with his friend, Father Pierre Bastain, in the next village. You will find him there.' He spoke at last, sulkily. 'And you will forgive my mentioning, madame, I do not admire your taste.'

Without a word, Marie turned to the door and hurried to her awaiting carriage. It was only a short journey to Father Bastain's presbytery and she spent the time deliberating on the fact that here was confirmation of all she had feared. Here was the vindication of her journey. Father Michel had been ousted from the parish he had served for so many years. Persecution of priests was not a Parisian phenomenon, as she had conjectured. Anti-clericalism had been prevalent in the rural parts of France for many years, but the revolution had brought a new dimension to it. Father Michel was indeed in danger. Well, this would but add weight to the arguments she would use; he *must* be persuaded to leave France, immediately. It might be that there would be insufficient time for her self-imposed plan, to defend the king. If that was so, it was a pity. Nevertheless, she smiled; it was clear where she must choose. Where the two men needed her, she must think first of the one she had loved first and longest.

Father Bastain was as much surprised by the arrival of the visitor from Paris as Father Gaudin had been — but much more gentlemanly. He explained that his friend was at present out of the house, walking in the fields.

'He often does so, madame. It wards off the melancholy, you understand.' He sighed. 'He feels the time hanging heavily on his hands, now he is forbidden to serve the Mass.' He shook his head, perplexed, and confided in her that he was afraid, too, that his friend disliked being dependent on his charity, living as a perpetual guest in his house. 'Though it is both my duty and pleasure to exercise Christian charity,' continued the kind old priest. 'For fear of imposing on my charity, he keeps out of the house for much of the day. I am indeed poor company for one of his intellect. Though he does not say, so, I would not have you think that, madame. No, I would not have you think I accuse him of deliberately distancing himself. It is simply that he is a solitary man, as perhaps you know. It is very possible he needs time to be alone with God.'

While he spoke the old priest bustled about, offering bread and milk to Marie, such poor hospitality as his home afforded. She, meanwhile, sat in the window seat, half attending to the garrulous old priest, yet with most of her attention rivetted on the gate of the field, restlessly awaiting Father Michel's return. At last she jumped to her feet.

'He comes, Father. He is approaching the gate now. I shall go to meet him.'

'By all means, madame,' came the benign reply. But Marie was already outside the door. She watched Father Michel walking across the field. He had not seen her yet. He looked older she thought, thinner, more careworn than she remembered. He looked down at the stubble beneath his feet. Then he lifted his eyes and saw her. He smiled and held out his hands.

'You here, Marie?' He took her hands in his.

'Yes, I have travelled to warn you of the events in Paris,' began Marie, without preamble. 'Father you cannot realise how far feeling has turned against priests. Why, only a week ago, I witnessed the most horrible slaughter. I shudder to recall it. I was distributing pamphlets in the *Rue de Seine,* you understand, when I saw...'

'You have not written to me for more than a year, Marie,' he interrupted, reproachfully. 'I have been anxious about you, wondering if you were continuing your foolhardy support for the king.'

'But it is *I,* Father, who feels such concern for *you!* I did write, in fact. I did not know of your dismissal from Pont d'Herault. You would not have received the letter, unless that insufferable young man there had troubled to deliver it.' Recalling the contents of the letter, her brief dismissal of Father Michel's interest in her, she added, 'Now I am glad he did not. It is of no importance now.'

'You have met Father Gaudin? You disliked him?' He sounded as if the thought pleased him.

'Yes, but that is also of no importance! Father, you must listen. You must leave France. There is no place of safety for priests such as you, who have repudiated the constitution. See, you are driven from your home, even in so obscure a place as this.' She continued with even greater urgency. 'You will say that you lack the means to flee, but that need not hinder you. I will supply the money. You need not scruple to take it, for I shall come with you. Together, we will leave France. It will be perfectly simple, you will see. We must not delay, however, but make all arrangements as speedily as possible, for you cannot understand...'

'I cannot understand what you speak of, Marie!' interrupted Father Michel, in great astonishment. 'I? To leave France in your company? You must know I could never do so!'

'But those who have been priests are in great danger, Father. This persecution, this massacre I saw in Paris. It was not an isolated incident, I am sure. I do not believe it will stop there.'

'No more do I, my dear,' he replied, calmly. 'But I shall not heed it. And do not speak of *those who have been priests,*' I beg of you Marie. It is a great sadness to me that the pope did not see fit to agree to the constitution of France, yes, I acknowledge that. But I have been a priest all my life. I cannot see myself in any other way.'

'But that is not the only way to know God. There is new thinking about religion itself, in Paris. I have come to tell you of it. If only you were there you would understand the enlightenment of these ideas, the idea that there is but one Supreme Being.' She rattled on, breathlessly. 'It is the idea that consciousness of God is innate within the heart and soul of every man and woman. That it is natural for men and women to seek the Ultimate Mystery within the depths of their own being. That what is ultimately real is beyond the God of the church. What is real is *Being Itself.* They speak of the supremacy of being.'

'This is the wisdom of your philosophers, Marie, I know.' He sighed and continued slowly and sorrowfully. 'Perhaps, after all, they are right. I do not know, any more. France has rejected the Church of Rome. The church has rejected me. But I, Marie, cannot change.'

'You can, you *shall,* with God's help, and with mine!'

'No, my dear child. To me, you are a child, with your enthusiasm... and your unquenchable hope. For me it is different. I am much older than you, remember. I am too old to change.'

'Father, you are not old, and you are man. Many men who have been priests have now become the men God intended them to be.' She looked deeply into her eyes and he returned her gaze.

'I know of what you speak. Do you not know how much I want to take you in my arms, now, this very minute? Do you not know that I have long wanted to do so? But I shall not, my dear love. For, you see, now I simply cannot. My very self has been the priesthood.'

She thought about this, thought about the identity most of us take for granted. Thought about her many identities, bastard child, reluctant wife, courtesan, writer. Throughout his life there had been only one way of being.

'I would be no one, nothing, if I escaped from France with you, Marie. I should be ashamed of my very being. Do not speak to me of a "Supreme Being" and yet seek to take my very being from me.' She was silent, the tears welled in her eyes at his refusal, yet she understood. He continued, more cheerfully.

'We are nevertheless a well matched pair! You will not listen to me, nor I to you. Let us talk of you, Marie, for I am troubled, as ever, by your impetuous ways. Have you ceased to support the king? It is a foolish and dangerous errand.'

'I shall endeavour to defend him, nonetheless.' Now her tears were flowing, in pity for the king, for the priest and for herself. 'He is defenceless, Father Michel. It is something I can try to do. He needs me, or one like me. You do not.'

'I have not said so.'

'You will not leave France in my company.'

'That, no. Call it, if you will, my sanctimonious fear of the scandal. Though it is not that, or that only in a small part.' There was a long silence. 'And yet I feel I shall be with you ere long, Marie.'

'Where, Father, when?'

'You will see, Marie. I shall come to you, if you need me. I am an insignificant man who has been merely a priest. You are well-known in Paris and have already aroused the enmity of the revolutionary extremists. You have put all your faith in what men and women can achieve. Always, that is very little. Always, their motives are a mixture of good and evil. I ask you to do one thing for me now.'

'I will, if it is possible.'

'Come to the church with me. Come and pray to God, or God by whatever name you chose to call Him. Come and pray with me.'

Together, silently, hand in hand, they walked to the church of Our Lady of Sorrows.

November, 1792 -Father Michel's Story – continued

My hands are idle, these hands which all my life I have kept with great care, because they have performed the miracle of consecration. I am forbidden to celebrate the Mass now. My whole life is idle, wasted. I am a pauper, living in hiding on the charity of the good priest, Father Bastain. Is he a good priest, I ask myself? He has taken the oath of allegiance to the Civil Constitution of France, where I have refused. Therefore he remains a priest, while I am no one, nothing. I do not know if he is a good priest. I do know, of his charity and Christian kindness, he is a good man.

    I confess I was dismayed when in April of last year, the papal bull condemned the Civil Constitution. I had hoped, until the last, that Pope Pius would have seen the need to reform the French Church. There should be more involvement of the people, and the church should be governed by the whole company of its pastors, not just powerful bishops. But the revolution has gone too far, it proposes nothing less than the secularization of the church. They say that in Paris there was great anger among the people when it was at last known that the pope denounced the Civil Constitution. The mob made effigies of him, and carried out mock executions, parading the straw heads of the pope through the streets on pikes. Here in the country it is different. The people are confused, they know not what to think or how to act. The Mass was an ingrained ritual in their lives. They did not always come to church, although on the day when I was expected to make my oath to the constitution they came in droves. Still the church was always there. The bells would sound on Sunday mornings; it is as if I can still hear the sound of the bells on winter mornings, their notes seemed to hang on the frosty branches of the trees, calling the people to worship. I would watch the trail of people ascending the hill to the church, reluctantly, perhaps, but obediently. It was their custom to do so. Now the bells are silent. What, I wonder, will become of the people of France, severed from the Church of Rome? I fear that by throwing out the church along with the monarchy, there will be a spiritual desert in France. There will be no recovery from this.

Much of the time I am preoccupied with my own turmoil. The Mass gave structure, meaning, purpose to my life. Now there is nothing. The rock on which I built my life has been shattered and destroyed. Could my life have been otherwise? I do not think so. I was destined to become a priest. My mother wished it so, and I shared her wishes. It would never have occurred to me to oppose my mother. Every day I have to remember that I am no longer a priest. Every day the loss is new to me. No one who has not performed the miracle of consecration can know what a void is left in life when it is gone. It is as if the soul has been wrenched from me. I am no one, nothing.

Last year I wrote to Marie Gouze, warning her that her support for the king would endanger her. I feared for her, since I love her. This I confess to myself. I confess also that I was jealous of her worship for Louis XVl. I had become accustomed to the knowledge of her carnal life for many years but that was in the past. This was different. I had come to believe that her respect and confidence were reserved for me, her former tutor. Then she came to visit me in the most extraordinary way, after the massacre of the priests in Paris, two months ago. She feared for me, just as I fear for her. Our feelings for each other were as one. But she made the most impulsive suggestion, that we should flee together from France. I could not do so, of course. The idea was scandalous, outrageous. But yet, what should prevent me? Many men who have been priests have married since the revolution. In any case, I am no longer a priest. But I am a pauper. How could I depend on a wealthy woman for money? I did not tell her that my objections were concerned with money; I had a man's pride. I talked instead of the scandal and the impossibility of changing my life. I did not tell her that I yearned to go with her; a great part of my soul wanted to agree to her plan. I wanted to go with her, wanted to because I love her. That is when I first thought, could my life have been different? Our lives are very circumstantial, and into my life came Marie Gouze, to torment me, yet also to love me. That I know, and how can I regret her love, since I return it? This I acknowledge to myself, at last. I first knew when she came to Pont d'Herault on the day designated for priests to take the oath to the constitution, two years ago. There in the sacristy of the church, I would have loved her in the flesh. There is something in her which draws me like a magnet. I tell myself that it is a magnetism of the spirit, two souls in harmony, yet I know it is earthly, also. We are like one spirit split in two parts, but there is an urge, a feeling that these two parts should be united, as Christ is united with his church. Except that this also is no longer so, not in France.

I am a disunited soul, in harmony with nothing and no one. I cry to God as Job cried to him; where are you now? Why have you forsaken me, who has resisted temptation for so many years? Marie talked to me wildly, during her last visit, of the Supreme Being. All my life I have believed one can only know the God who is revealed by the church. But now the church has also forsaken me. Man cannot construct God. But perhaps God himself is a construct of the mind of man. If the edifice of the church crumbles, perhaps another faith must be fashioned in its place. I do not know, but I know it is all too late for me. After I talked with Marie, we walked together to the church, hand in hand. Then we knelt and prayed silently. We prayed for each other, I have no doubt, no more than I doubt our mutual love. But otherwise I believe our prayers were different. Marie believes in free will. She will have prayed for the triumph of the revolution, for liberty, equality and the brotherhood and sisterhood of men and women. She is a free spirit. Her life has been a series of choices, very brave choices, I admit, even though I have not always approved of them. My life has been different. My life has been predetermined. I have not acted from any sense of free will. I have believed this determinism has been driven by Divine Will. But when I look at the desolation in France I wonder, who has determined the events which are shaping our history? Men and women are killing each other in the streets of Paris and in the country, in thousands. I cannot believe they consciously choose to do so. I cannot believe they know what they are doing. Who wills it? Who is in control? I believe there is nothing in control in an unthinking universe.

I am fifty-seven years old. For the first time in my life, I doubt my faith. Despair is, I believe, the greatest of sins, but I know not what I should do. I am accustomed to a solitary life, but I have never felt alone as I do now. This is strange, for I am living for the first time with another person, with Father Bastain. I fear I am a poor companion for him, I cannot enter easily into idle chatter, the small exchanges of social intercourse. I have never been able to do so. I walk daily in the fields as I have always done, but in the past my mind was tranquil, it was filled with prayer. Now my walks are desolate and my thoughts a quagmire of uncertainty. I was accustomed to pray as I walked, but now I cannot pray. My mind is filled with a turmoil of thoughts of Marie Gouze. Solitary thought is tormenting, but I find I cannot help myself from thinking, could I have been a man, as other men? Could I have been her lover?

1792-1793 Pierre's Story, continued

My mother has become a cursed meddler, an infernal liability. It was bad enough when she was writing her gibberish about the rights of women under the new constitution of France, and publishing her absurd plays, championing the rights of the colonial slaves. One could laugh at the rantings of a mere woman. But now she involves herself in serious political issues. She has claimed to love me, to have furthered my career, but she has no understanding of the difficulties of an officer in the French army in these uncertain times. It was she, after all, who promoted my military career, but she does not think of the consequences of her foolish writing. I am an officer in the army under the command of Dumouriez and a respectably married man. A notorious mother who involves herself in the politics of France is quite inappropriate for me, and detrimental to my interests.

In April 1792, the French declared war on Austria. For a time all went well. Dumouriez, with forty thousand men, was victorious at Valmy and Jemappes. We entered Brussels in triumph, to the sound of bells ringing. But these victories were shortlived. The army was defeated at Neerwinden in March of the following year. Dumouriez defected to the Austrians. Well, I can't say I blame him for his so-called treason, every man must look to his own interests in these troublesome times. But I do blame my mother for treating the war as if it is a great event in the cause of revolutionary freedom, some sort of theatrical drama. She wrote a pamphlet which read:

Look how the generous host of France's most brilliant youth fly to our frontiers, there to shed their pure and stainless blood. And for whom, great heavens? For the Fatherland.

If this is meant to be a flattering reference to me, it fails. It merely shows how little understanding my mother has. Soldiering is a man's job, and it is an officer's task to obey orders from his commanders and to give orders to his subordinates, to make sure the task is carried out. Revolutionary ideals have nothing to do with it. But, most foolishly, my mother has allied herself with the Girondins, who supported the king. Could they, and she, not see that the cause of Louis XV1 was hopelessly lost? She calls herself a champion of the revolution, but she shows a complete lack of political acumen. Her most recent broadsheet is called *Les Trois Urnes*. It is absurd beyond belief. Its full title is *The Three Urns, or the Salvation of the Fatherland by an Aerial Traveller.* Who is this Aerial Traveller? Some sort of Angelic courtesan? Herself, perhaps, for she is incurably vain. In this broadsheet she proposes a choice among three forms of government. Unbelievably, all citizens are to be permitted to vote in this national plebiscite, all, *including female citizens!* How does she imagine women have the intelligence to understand politics? She herself demonstrates their complete inability to do so. I wish she had stayed earning her living by lying on her back. The bedchamber is the place for women. Fortunately, my wife understands this well. Her role in life is to please me, and to provide me with legitimate children. She has fulfilled her duty admirably, had she not done so, I would have known how to master her with the end of a rope. Women do not understand affairs of government but they understand mastery in a man.

The first suggestion in my mother's ridiculous broadsheet is an indivisible republic. The second, a federal government. The third, even more absurdly, a constitutional monarchy. Constitutional monarchy is an impossibility, of course, since Louis XV1 laid his head on the block on January 21st 1793. They say he went to his execution with courage, mounting the scaffold in *La Place de la Liberte* with great calm and dignity. That is as may be, he showed himself unable to rule France in his lifetime, and my mother's support for him has done her no favours. More importantly, it has endangered my position. Her second suggestion, federalism, is anathema to the Jacobins and they are in the ascendancy in these troubled times. The days of the Girondins are numbered, and I strongly suspect, my mother's days will be numbered along with them. For, two days after the execution of the king, her so called republican play *L'Entree de Dumouriez a Bruxelles* was performed at the Theatre de la Republique. What execrable timing and what a ridiculously unfortunate play! In this play Dumouriez, with the Duc de Chartres, appears in a triumphant entry to Brussels, hailed by the Belgian soldiers as a revolutionary hero. French soldiers are depicted as fraternizing with the citizens of Brussels, spreading the message of the revolution. What nonsense! As if soldiers are interested in revolutionary ideals or the spouting of *les philosophes!* The so-called play was the product of my mother's romantic and distorted imagination, and utterly ridiculous. I heard afterwards that the play was badly received and at the end of the first night she announced herself as the author. She would have done better to sneak out quietly, disguising her identity, for all she did was provoke laughter and derision. The second performance was even worse, from all accounts. The audience leapt on the stage and danced the *Carmagnole*. Worse was to follow for, as I say, my mother has no sense of timing and even less of political expediency. Two months later, the army was defeated at Neerwinden. So much for the glory of Dumouriez! Instead of being the hero of the Girondins he was the ignominious traitor, and again I say, I wager the fortunes of the Girondins will go down with him. In these times, it is vital to keep one's wits about one and to back the winning horse as the race changes course. My mother has the most unfortunate tendency to back losers. Yet she thinks of herself as a politician! My children, though still in the schoolroom, would have more sense.

The scenes in Paris have been most exciting, they say, and I am only sorry to have missed most of them while I was fighting in Austria for the lost cause of the French army. I am a soldier and, naturally, I am fired by bloodshed and thoughts of death. There can be no greater excitement, not even the excitement of the bedchamber. You see the enemy on the other side of the line. It is an invisible line of course, the line between life and death, to kill or to be killed. And you want to cross that line, to meet your fate, and yet of course at the same time you dread crossing it because it is a step into the unknown. Just as we shall all, someday, cross the line between life and death, so for the soldier that is the excitement of every day on the field of battle. And just before crossing the line everything is vivid, the blue sky with clouds scudding across it, the rays of sunlight on the fields, the rabbit poking its head from the burrow. You see the world differently. The excitement gets into your blood, there is nothing to compare with it.

For most of 1793 there was great sport in *La Place de la Revolution,* so named after the death of Louis XV1. People would gather together in their thousands to see what they called the Red Mass, barging and fighting for the front seats with *Trichodectes.* There would be wine and biscuits to buy from the hawkers and bread rolls to dip in the blood of the victims, savoury morsels, they must have been! While the people were drinking and brawling, others would place bets about the order the *huissers* would decide upon, for the prisoners to mount the scaffold. Then there were three sounds to listen for, in quick succession. The first would be the thud as the prisoner was thrown on the plank, the second thud would be the placing of the neck clamp on the victim, then there would be the glorious, swishing rattle as the heavy blade of the guillotine fell. Then there would be more betting, as to how many the guillotine would polish off in an hour. A marvellous invention, indeed! All the time, the writhing, quivering corpses would be mounting up and people would drink until they were merry enough to leap up and dance the *Carmagnole* on the top of the heap of bodies. That must have been the most hilarious part, for one can imagine the difficulty of keeping on one's legs on the slippery mountain of flesh! It must have been an art to stay upright, but as I say, sadly I missed most of it.

I was told that sometimes, if it was a special prisoner, there would be special treatment. The Princess de Lamballe, who, they said, was a bedfellow of the queen, was executed early on, before *La Famille Capet,* as the king and queen had been styled. She got the best treatment of all. She was stripped and raped and then her legs were spread well apart and nailed down, so a fire could be lit between them. Then her head was cut off and carried on a pike to a nearby cafe, so the customers could drink a toast to her death. Afterwards it was paraded beneath the queen's window, to make sure she could see what had become of her dear lover. One has to admire the ingenuity of the revolutionaries. Mind you, I never did think much of what they called the revolutionary philosophy, all the talk of liberty, fraternity and equality. You don't have much in the way of liberty when you're strapped down, awaiting the services of Madame Guillotine, do you? As I have said, I don't have a high opinion of women, but it was a woman who pointed this out. This was Manon Roland, and I *did* get to see her execution. Truth to tell, she was quite a cosy armful, I noticed, before they strapped her to the plank. When she was ready, nicely strapped in, she looked up to the statue of Liberty which had been erected in *La Place de la Revolution,* and said, loudly and clearly,

'Oh Liberty, what crimes are committed in your name!'

Well, I wouldn't call the executions crimes, but I took her point. The revolution didn't bring very much in the way of liberty. Though one excellent result has been the dechristianisation of France. As I have said before, I have never had much time for women, and even less for the clergy. In October 1793 the Commune ordered the closure of all the churches in the city. Some were converted to Temples of Reason. There were ceremonies where folk danced before the sanctuary, howling the *Carmagnole.* Men stripped off their breeches and women went naked from the waist, there would be a fine bouncing of breasts to the music of the horn before they got down to copulation in the sacristy. There was no end of sport, croziers were used as drum majors' staffs and genuflected to the comeliest women, making mockery of the manners of priests. I wonder what my mother's dear friend, Father Michel Dupre, would make of it all? That is, if he is still alive. There is good reason to believe he may be dead. Of this I will write no more. Many priests have been butchered and good riddance to them, say I.

    The important thing for me is to disassociate myself from my mother. I must look to my own interests and do whatever is necessary to secure my safety and the safety of my family. I do not feel any loyalty to my mother, nor any pity for her. She has brought these troubles upon herself by her absurd meddling in matters she does not understand. I expect, at any time, to hear of her arrest, but, I repeat, I will not support her. I owe her nothing.

1793 Arrest and Meeting in the Prison of L'Abbaye

After her meeting with Father Michel in Pont d'Herault, Marie sank into an unaccustomed depression. It was the end of her hopes that a future with Michel Dupre could become reality. She should have known that this vision was a fantasy. Always, she had lived in a world of fantasy and unreality, refusing to be bogged down by anything as tiresome and mundane as being real. And yet she persuaded herself that her hopes were practical, that they could be realised. But he could not be moved. For herself, she believed, had always believed, that life could change, that she was in control of her destiny and could influence the destinies of others. Her nature was buoyant. Thus, her despondency was lifted by the news that, at last, the Constituent Assembly had legalised divorce on equal terms for men and women. The grounds included incompatibility, mutual consent, and the desertion of one spouse by another for a period of two years. She herself had been freed from the married state for many years, since the death of Louis Aubry. She shuddered, still, at the recollection of her early marriage. During the first year of legal divorce, it was estimated that more than three thousand couples took advantage of the new laws. Marie reflected on the fact that, in reality, the law very much favoured men. Few women had the economic power to leave their husbands, or the courage to do so without financial means. This would always be so, until women had the right to express themselves politically. A substructure of political equality was essential, she believed, for women to strive for opportunities of economic independence. There must be employment which would allow them to stand on their feet instead of lying on their backs. Thus, with her accustomed enthusiasm and in a brave effort to clear her thoughts of her hopeless love, she took up her pen.

This welcome legislation must be underpinned by political equality for women, for only then will the spirit of the law be achievable. Equal rights in divorce are impossible without equal employment opportunities for women. They need the political power to fight for them.

Her ideas magnified as she envisaged a fair and free solution for the future of France. She wrote on, with mounting excitement and idealism.

With equal political rights there can be a plebiscite to decide the future of France. This, we could perhaps call "Les Trois Urnes". The three urns of the title offer the choice of republican government, federal government or monarchy. Let the people choose, and by that I mean all the people, not just the men of France.

She was pleased with this idea, it was well-imagined, neat and just. The voice of women must be heard, for she was convinced that men were responsible for the bloodshed which was tainting the ideals of the revolution. Women were nurturers, they did not make war or descend to violence. She wrote on:

I greatly fear the ideology of the Revolution will be swamped in blood unless the tempering voice of women is soon allowed to be heard. We must save the life of the king; the honour of France demands it. We condemn Robespierre, Marat and others who portray themselves as incorruptible yet in reality seek personal aggrandizement. These men we hold responsible for the bloodshed which is besmirching the achievements of the Revolution. Why must it be so, that our ideals are tainted with blood? The Revolution was born on the principles of liberty, fraternity and equality. I fear, I greatly fear, my friends, that our ideology will be ground into the dust, and history will remember only the terror of the Revolution, rather than the ideals for which we may be justly proud. I am a true Frenchwoman, proud that my country should lead the way to a greater, more enlightened civilization than the World has yet known. I trust in the principles of the National Convention. I know that my voice will not go unheard.

Marie's voice did not go unheard. Three days later, her suggestions, which she had printed and placarded through Paris, were greeted with a storm of abuse from an angry crowd of market women who gathered outside her apartment. She heard the raucous voices of the women as she sat in her boudoir, grooming *Voltaire* and *Rousseau*. It pained her that it should be women's voices that she heard. Her pamphlets had called for their voices, as lovers of peace and temperance.

'Who does she think she is, to meddle in such matters?'

'Why does she not knit stockings for our brave soldiers, instead of interfering in the affairs of men?'

'Seize the whore! A slap round the face with one of my flounders may cool her head,' cried one of the fishwives. Bawdy laughter greeted this.

'Take her and sit her in one of the market barrows. I've a

fine stock of rotten tomatoes and lettuce this day. She may like a face full of salad to whet her appetite!'

Marie remained calm. 'I shall go down and speak to the women,' she told Honorine.

'You cannot, madame. You will assuredly be killed!' cried her maid. In her frenzy she gripped her mistress' arm.

'Nonsense, Honorine.' Marie put her aside gently. They are women. I am one of them. To be sure they are foolish and uneducated. The more reason why I must speak with them.'

Her appearance at the door, her air of calm, provoked the crowd of angry women still further. One of the fishwives seized her by the hair and dragged off the lace cap she was wearing.

'What have I here?' she demanded of the delighted crowd. 'The head of Olympe de Gouges!' She thrust the cap onto her own head and paraded round. With a silly grin on her face, she kicked up her heels in the revolutionary dance. Then she snatched off the cap and cried,

'Tis time for the auction! Who will bid me ten sous for the head of Olympe de Gouges?'

Marie remained unperturbed. She answered gaily. 'My friend, I'll bid you twenty, and I demand the first refusal!' She smiled serenely. 'Come, sisters, cease your play acting. There are important matters ahead and we must speak of them. Come into my apartment now, that we may speak together. Come, those of you who see yourselves as leaders. I beg you to come.'

So she invited a dozen of the ringleaders into her drawing room, and there, regardless of their dirt, she sat them down and personally attended to them, bringing wine and cakes. Then she talked with them. So the ugly incident passed away. But there were other occasions of abuse, to Honorine's growing alarm. Marie remained maddeningly untroubled. It was unfortunate, she agreed, that the people, particularly the women, seemed impervious to the logic of her arguments, did not seem to see that their lives would remain degraded until they, along with their menfolk, were empowered politically. Clearly, great patience was needed in trying to educate the women, and patience was not a virtue she had ever possessed in great measure. Nevertheless she persisted, whenever the mob hailed her from beneath the balcony in the Rue de Rivoli, humouring, gaily cajoling, seemingly tireless in her efforts to persuade the women to understand what to her was so clear. On one occasion, however, she was very much shaken and turned abruptly away from the balcony, shutting the windows firmly and closing the shutters. She had been engaged with a particularly raucous crowd, both men and women. White and trembling, she sank into a chair. Honorine came to her.

'What ails you, madame? There now, I told you not to bandy words with the mob. It is not fitting for you, and see now, I was right. You are unwell. You will kill yourself, I believe, thinking and writing and talking to these pestilential people who do not know what is good for them. Come, lie down now and rest...'

'Honorine, I am very well. Just a little tired. Please leave me now.'

'Nonsense, m'lady. You must let me help you to undress and take you to your bed.'

'No, no please.' Marie spoke with decision. 'I want simply to be alone. Please go as I ask you.'

She sat motionless in the chair, staring blankly at the

closed shutters. She was quite alone, apart from *Voltaire*, who circled around her legs and then slumped to the floor, utterly relaxed, draping his elegant paws over her feet. Outside, she could still hear the shouts and bawls of the crowd, now fading into the distance, for since she had declined to continue the debate, they were moving on to a new sparring match. She couldn't, she couldn't be quite sure, but she thought she had seen him. There at the back of the crowd, silent, not calling out lewd comments like the other men, but menacingly silent, she had seen a thickset young man who she believed was her son, Pierre. It was more than a year since she had seen him. Had he, then, returned from his duties with the army? If so, why had he not come to her? Why was he there with the mob, outside her window? The man had stared at her with eyes like a wolf, and a devilish sneer on his face. Surely it could not be Pierre? It was a large crowd, and that kind of young soldier was a commonplace type in Paris. Perhaps she had been mistaken. She must have imagined it was her son. Still shuddering, but resolutely dismissing the matter from her mind, she returned to her writing and became once again absorbed in her work.

Three days later, two police commissioners with a group of national guardsmen demanded entry to her apartment. They ransacked her drawers and seized the documents from her writing desk. She was immediately taken to the prison of L'Abbaye.

The prison of L'Abbaye was not austere. Marie had a small room of her own, and a bed. To be sure, the mattress was not of the pure down she had grown accustomed to, but still, she would have been moderately comfortable were it not for the walls of her cell, which were permanently damp. She shivered constantly, her teeth chattering in her head, as if she had a fever. A sour-looking, taciturn woman brought her meals at regular intervals, bread, wine and a little meat. She firmly refused the meat. She was told, grudgingly, by the maid, that she was allowed the freedom to roam the prison during the daytime, and even to walk in the small, high-walled garden at the back, if she chose. However, for the first few days, Marie was too shocked, too stunned by the sheer injustice of her imprisonment, to take heed of her surroundings. It was a dreadful mistake, a grotesque iniquity. She had believed passionately in the rights of the people of France and had spent several years struggling to find words which would promote them. How, in the name of liberty, fraternity and equality, could this be done to her? She was so struck by the ridiculous nature of her situation, so filled with righteous anger, that she was completely unafraid. What was there to fear, when she had done nothing wrong?

From the start of her imprisonment, Marie was denied her legal right to a lawyer, on the grounds that she was more than capable of defending herself. She was unperturbed; this was clearly true, and at least the judgement showed regard for her powers of oratory and persuasion. Her self-esteem was appeased. She neither needed nor desired a lawyer, for she was guiltless. No jury in the land could find her guilty of a crime, when she had committed none.

After a few days, her vanity asserted itself. She summoned the maid and asked for a mirror, grimacing ruefully when she looked in the small square of glass the maid brought her. She was pale from want of food, and her hair hung in dishevelled tangles around her shoulders. Marie had grown unaccustomed to waiting on herself, but she managed to rectify the damage done to her person by days of inner rage and outer inertia. Then she sallied forth to make a wider inspection of her surroundings.

What she saw appalled her. In a distant wing of the prison, only reached by a long walk through a labyrinth of corridors, men and women were herded together in large empty rooms. The walls were not whitewashed and the floors were strewn with evil smelling straw. As she stared through the iron bars, the feelings of pity aroused in her were stifled by a more primitive physical repulsion. The air was foetid with the smell of human excrement and the effluvia of the sick. At least a dozen people were lying half naked on the straw, shaking with typhus or racked with the lung-bursting coughing of the last stages of consumption. The plaintive eyes of some of the prisoners who stared dumbly at her, spoke more eloquently than words. Some were simply dying of hunger.

Nauseous, she turned away and hurried in what she thought was the direction of her own cell. She was quickly lost. The prison was a maze of dark passageways. Turning one corner, she found herself in the brutal clasp of a lascivious old prisoner.

'Make an old man happy, my pretty?' He grinned at her. She said nothing, but tore herself away. Turning a corner, she found herself confronted by a man and woman prisoner, lying on the floor in the act of fornication. This was permitted, it seemed, in a prison which nevertheless saw fit to starve the prisoners and deprive them of the most rudimentary medical care. At last, finding the corridor to her own room by chance, she hurried there, gasping for breath as she ran. She rang the bell in a frenzy of impatience to summon the maid. Arlette, the serving woman came shuffling into the room, her arms folded across her ample chest.

'Well?' she asked, moodily.

'I have just come from the other side of the prison,' announced Marie. 'I am shocked beyond belief. I cannot understand why the prisoners are living in such conditions. They lie worse than dogs or swine. I would not leave animals in conditions such as these! The maid shrugged indifferently.

'You have your quirks, madame.'

'But why are they living in such a way? Answer me, woman.' Marie stamped her foot in anger.

'It is nothing to me, and not my concern,' responded the maid, in flat ones. 'But the reason, if you would have one, is simple. You have money. You can pay. They cannot. Your servants have supplied the prison authorities with money for your comforts.'

'And this is so, even since the revolution, which speaks of equality!' cried Marie.

'That is your trouble, madame, if I may say so. You think too much of the revolution. The revolution is nothing.'

'And what is their crime, these people? Are they, perhaps, violent offenders?'

'Their crime, as I tell you, is that they cannot pay. They are debtors.'

'Merely debtors? Is it a crime, then to be poor?' The servant laughed scornfully.

'The greatest crime of all, and it will always be so. There is no more serious crime, madame. That is why they are here, and that is why they are confined in the way you see.' She walked out of the room.

Marie's sense of anguish overcame her for several minutes. She circled the room like a caged tigress in her wrath, clasping her hands to her temples. Then abruptly, she stopped, seized the bell, and rung it up and down until its clatter echoed along the corridors. Arlette's measured, unhurried tread could be heard approaching the door.

'What is it now?' demanded the servant, with scarcely-veiled insolence.

'Bring me paper and pen and ink, immediately, my good woman. There are matters I must write about!'

'And I must warn you, madame. I have orders that everything you write must be passed to the proper authorities. It matters not to me, *bien sur*. But if you take my advice you will write nothing.'

'Nonsense, woman! There are things I must make known, about these evil conditions. The legislative assembly must be informed.'

Arlette laughed derisively.

'You think the authorities do not know? You think they would care? You are a foolish woman, for all your writing. Each word you write will tighten the noose around your neck and will hammer yet another nail in your coffin. Writing! Pah! I am glad I am an unlettered woman.'

Marie scarcely listened to her and was quite unmoved by this grim foreboding. There was simply no time to argue with the stupid creature, when there was work to be done. She, Olympe de Gouges, had done nothing wrong, after all. It was impossible that anyone should say so. So she wrote in haste to

Honorine, begging her to send more money, immediately, to supply the needs of the poor indebted prisoners of L'Abbaye.

*L'Abbaye Prison
August, 1793*

I cannot describe to you the plight of the prisoners, and will not delay in doing so, ma chere amie. It is of greater importance that I make known these conditions to the legislative assembly. You must take all the money you will find in the drawer of my boudoir, and deliver it to the prison gates in my name, that I may buy what is needed for the poor prisoners. I would ask you to inform all who know me, and may care, of my imprisonment. It seems I am allowed to have visitors, but pray do not come yourself, ma chere, for you would cry and scold me for what I do, and that I could not bear. Instead, take care of my affairs, as you have always done. The living here is very free, and much of my time is spent in warding off the unwelcome attentions of male prisoners. I am allowed much freedom, but no news, and am sadly out of touch with political affairs. Life here resembles a human pond. There is much activity within, much coupling and breeding, but no awareness of the outside world. So, dear Honorine, do not come to me , but write to tell me of the progress of the Revolution. Kiss Voltaire and Rousseau for me.

*Your friend and mistress,
Marie Gouze.*

Then she turned her attention to the urgent matter which troubled her and wrote an impassioned article, condemning the conditions of the prison and addressing the matter to the legislative assembly, for their immediate attention. Eventually it was received by the assembly, and greeted with derisive laughter by the deputies, who said, 'It is merely Olympe de Gouges, that troublesome woman.' But some began to mutter. The woman interfered too much.

Two months passed. Each day Marie crossed to the other side of the prison with baskets of rolls and passed them through the bars, smiling serenely at the poor depraved creatures whose clawing fingers clutched them eagerly. She had no visitors, saw no one from the outside world. Then, one cold autumn morning, as the dank mists were beginning to seep into the prison walls, she sat shivering in her cell when the maid Arlette brought her bread and wine.

'There is a man to see you. Well, I suppose he passes for a man. A priest, in fact. I'm surprised at you, madame, you who prate and preach of the revolution, that you should need the services of one who follows the whore of Rome.'

'Need the services?' enquired Marie, bemused by this announcement. 'I require no services from a priest. I have not requested any. Why should I?'

'Nevertheless a priest demands to see you and says he has travelled far.'

'What is his name?'

'He gives no name. Shall I send him in then? Myself, I would not speak with such a one, but then, I am not in the kind of extremity in which you find yourself, madame.'

The irritating prisoner, however, failed as usual to comprehend her insinuations and merely replied, 'Please do.'

The visitor stood for several moments at the doorway, just

looking at her. She looked, smaller, whiter, more frail than he remembered. Yet still beautiful. Then, as he walked towards her she burst into speech.

'Father Michel! I did not think to see you here, to visit me in such a place! Why, I believe it is the very first time you have been in Paris, always I have visited you in the country. Such a pity I am not at home in my apartment. You have never seen my apartment I think, after all the years I have lived in Paris? To think that I am not at home, to show you all there is to see in the city! It is an unfortunate mistake, *n'est ce pas,* that I am here? Though I should not complain, for the situation of many people here is more than unfortunate. It is scandalous! Let me tell you of the conditions some prisoners are housed in. I must tell you, since you *are* here, for you may be able to help. For I have written often and often to the assembly, and I fear my letters are going astray, for there has been no inspection and nothing changes. Perhaps I could charge you with the safe delivery of some letters, Father Michel. The prison authorities seem careless of such things. That is, of course, if you are making a long stay in Paris. How strange to see you here, after all! *C'est amusant, n'est ce pas?* Well, I cannot go about the city with you, just at present, which is a great pity, but perhaps it is more important that I show you what I *can* show you, and that is the plight of some of the poor prisoners here. I am spending all my resources on food for them, to keep them from starvation. It is not of course that I begrudge it, but even so…'

At last he broke in, saying with exasperation, 'Marie, do you not realise you must die?'

'Die?' she echoed blankly. There was silence. 'Well, of course I must, we all must, ultimately.' She laughed,

211

hysterically. 'It is so funny of you, Father, and so typical, to speak always of the next life, when there is so much to do in this one!'

'I mean, Marie, that you must die very soon.' He looked closely into her face. 'Is it possible you have not realised this?'

'Why should I? I am not ill. A little tired and weak, perhaps. But I am not ill.'

'Why do you think I have travelled so far to see you?'

'Indeed, as I say, it is a strange turn of events that you should do so. I wonder that you have been able to manage the journey for I know your stipend it is very small. Indeed since the Civil Constitution I suppose you have none. I am truly grateful for your coming, Father Michel and so glad to see you, for there is much to do to further the causes I care for so deeply.' Impassioned and perfervid, she tried to launch into further speech, but he interrupted her, bluntly.

'Marie, they will send you to the guillotine and they will do so soon. I have come for the good of your soul, which was ever dear to me, more dear, I believe, than my own.'

'No!' she shouted. Her face was chalk-white. 'Do not speak to me of such things. I am innocent. Not innocent of all sin, of course, not sinless in the way you would think. But innocent of crime against the people. This I am accused of, I who have done all in my power to help the people.'

'The revolution is not the people, Marie. At least, not any more.' He added, quietly, 'If it ever was.'

'I shall have a trial, I understand, and then, *naturellement,* this unfortunate captivity will be brought to an end. For there is nothing, *nothing,* you understand, for which they can say I am guilty.'

'You believe in justice?'

'Of course, who does not?'

'Listen to me, Marie,' he replied, urgent at last. 'Turn your mind to the justice of God. Forget that of men, for there is none. You have hoped too much for justice in this life, and it has brought you to this end.'

She was silent, so he continued more brutally.

'Do you not know? The king had a trial and then they brought him to the scaffold. He climbed the steps and then he laid his head on the block. He had no choice. Oh yes, he spoke fine words of innocence before he did so. But there was nothing he could do but lay his head on that block. So the blades of the guillotine descended and his head was severed from his body. They will do the same to the queen and they will do the same to you.'

'You really believe they will do this to me?' she answered, incredulously.

'I know it, my dear. That is why I am here. You have been a friend to the people, have fought with passion and vigour for their welfare. This I know. But you are an enemy of Robespierre and those men who now lead the revolution. They are bringing all France to a state of godlessness with their idea of the Supreme Being. It is they who see themselves as supreme. And I fear, I greatly fear, Marie, that *they are supreme, at least where your life is concerned.*'

'You say I must die? You say I put too much trust in men?' She repeated his words wonderingly, like a child repeating a lesson.

'Assuredly this is so, dear Marie. Now is the time to put your trust in God. Let me, just this once, at this most important time, hear your confession.'

Too shocked, too weak to resist his fervent pressure, she allowed herself to recite the formula of the confession, long unused yet still familiar. As she recited, like an automaton, she wondered that he knew so little, after so many years, of her state of mind, of her lack of faith, of her fear of death. Afterwards they sat in silence, their hands entwined. Then she spoke tentatively, seeking his understanding.

'It is knowing my death is fixed, I think, which makes me fearful.'

'My dear, we none of us know the hour or the day. That is why our souls must be in a state of readiness to meet God.'

'Yes, but I do know the hour of my death, at least, I suppose I shall. That, and the blood.' She shuddered, childhood memories flooding her mind.

'I imagine,' he replied, judiciously, wholly without imagination, 'that you will know nothing of the blood.'

She changed the subject, for she found she was shaking. Quietly and quite conversationally she asked, 'Do you think we two will meet again, Father, after we are both dead?'

'I believe so, I believe we will be together for all eternity, with God.'

How fortunate he was, to have such belief. He would not have to comfort himself with the cold comfort of reason, 'They say when I am dead I shall not know it.' But she dared not say this to him, dared not tread further on the tendrils of his faith. So she picked up his last words.

'Eternity? It is difficult to imagine it, Father.'

'Yes,' he conceded. 'That is because we know only time and think of eternity as endless time. But it is the antithesis of time, a condition in which time is no more. We who are in this mortal condition, we cannot imagine it. That is not to say it does not exist.'

She frowned and stood up. She walked over to the window and clutched the bars, staring out, trying to comprehend his meaning. Then she shook her head impatiently, as if trying to shake off a troublesome fly.

'No, that is no use to me, that idea. For I shall want to live in time until you come to me, Father Michel.' Two large tears welled in her eyes but she continued to stare out of the window, blindly. 'I shall miss you so,' she whispered softly.

He looked across at the small figure standing motionless at the window. She had turned her head as the tears coursed down her cheeks. From where he was sitting he saw her in profile, her defiant little nose with a large tear rolling down the side of it, her small breasts heaving. And suddenly a shroud was lifted from him as he realised the truth of what she had said. It was true, this is what her human loss would mean. Eternity? What comfort was the idea? She who had loved him since she was a child would be no more in the flesh. She would be gone from his life. Suddenly it mattered terribly. He realised with an awful clarity, why he had come to Paris. Not to hear the formula of her confession, not to comfort her, not to send her to God. He had come to claim her as his own.

Marie looked at him and read his eyes. The silence between them was terrible, as terrible as the silence of the bough of a tree, struck by lightning and about to snap. She knew what was meant by the intensity of that silence. She knew that he wanted her, truly wanted her at last. She looked at him and slowly loosened her clothing. The gown slipped away from her. She pulled the cord of her girdle and let it fall away. There she stood before him, Venus, Minerva and Juno together in his imagination for years, now together in Marie. She waited, motionless in the penetrating silence. The silence seemed like an eternity itself, though in reality it was merely a matter of seconds. Then she heard the creaking of the floorboards as he came towards her. She smiled enigmatically as she felt his lips on her eyelids. Her small hands tightened round his neck, claiming him as her own as he lifted her and carried her to the small pallet in the corner of the room. He tore off his clothes as he said, 'I must lose no more time, Marie. There is no time to waste since I love you so.'

Long afterwards they slept. Still in his arms, with her own arm trailing across his breast, she lay with her head on his shoulder. She wanted to look at him, to read his face, but she dared not move lest he should wake. So many thoughts crowded into her mind. She knew, now, what passion he was capable of, in impulse, and what potent execution of love would have been his, like his execution of the mass, had he had time to perfect it. She knew she had possessed his imagination, and held it, and held it at last to the end. She did not think that she loved him, absolutely and irrevocably, because that was a truth too certain for thought.

He lay still, his face like a beautiful effigy. At last he stirred and turned to her sleepily, his hand seeking hers.

'You regret?' asked Marie, timidly.

Father Michel smiled. 'Regret? No, *certainment non*. I feel as if I have never loved until now. *On n'aime q'une fois, la premiere*. It has taken me a lifetime to know that to love another person is to love God.'

Marie smiled also, that, being the man that he was, she must share his love with God. But nonetheless, his answer pleased and reassured her.

'For me also. I have loved you for so long. There have been many men in my bed, so many I cannot recall. But never a love such as this, a love that is more than a physical act. A love that is metaphysical, a love of the gods.'

She sighed, thinking that if only it could go on, if only she could escape death, how exquisitely beautiful, how rapturous their lives would be. But then, she comforted herself, human happiness is ephemeral, a matter of moments. Moments like this were rare, unique, beyond time. Timeless, yet eternal. She thought what he had said about time and eternity. Would she have this memory after death?

Father Michel turned to her. 'Marie, I have no regret. I love you and time is short. Come to me again.'

He was living in the present of his love as he took her in his arms again. She thought no more about time. It ceased for them as they loved.

Darkness was falling in the cell. Marie rose at last and walked to the small table where a single candle lay waiting to be lit. The shadows were lengthening as she lit the candle and said, gently, 'Michel, we have often misunderstood each other. Let us not do so now that there is so little time. Will you come to me again?' It was the first time she had addressed him without saying "Father".

'Assuredly my dearest love. How can you doubt? I shall come often, for it will be some time, I imagine, before the trial is completed.' Then he smiled and added, sardonically, 'After all, I am a priest. I must hear your confession.'

'Michel, never did I think to hear you making a joke about God.' She laughed as she embraced him and left him at the door.

Father Michel was deep in thought as he trudged in the direction of the lodging house where he had bespoken a room. Unfamiliar with the streets of Paris, he barely knew in which direction he walked, though he knew he must cross the Seine in order to reach the lodging house. Crossing a bridge, he stopped and stared at the swirling waters beneath him. His hands gripped the parapet until the knuckles were white. The clouds had parted and the last evening sunlight gleamed weakly. Beneath him the water was burnished in the evening light and the trees and bridges seemed to be etched beneath the surface of the water, leaf by leaf and line by line. It was that time of the evening light when all colours are enhanced.

As he gazed at the water beneath the bridge he thought of his past life, utterly devoted to the church which had rejected him, prelapsarian in its innocence. For the love of the Mother of God he had suppressed his manhood. He had spoken truthfully to Marie, he had no regrets and would assuredly return to her. But still, though he had been truthful, yet it was not the whole truth. His sense of self was disturbed, how could it not be, after such a life changing experience? He tried to say an act of contrition, but the words were hollow, meaningless. Simply, he could not be sorry for loving Marie.

Still staring down at the waters, now gleaming like oil, he composed his own prayer to meet the exigencies of the situation. His prayer was confused. 'Forgive me, Lord for breaking my vows, forgive me that my carnal love has brought me joy. How can such a love be wrong? Thank you for guiding me to love Marie at last. Help me to give her the love and strength she needs at this time.' For once, Mary the Mother of God found no place in his prayer, she was blurred, indistinct, formless. Instead, the white, marble breasts of Marie, Venus, Minerva and Juno rose like a beautiful vision in his mind. 'God help me,' he prayed, as his head sunk onto his hands, leaning over the parapet towards the darkening waters below.

Thus it was that he never saw his assassin. But a priest, flagrantly wearing his clerical garb in Paris in 1793 was an obvious target. The young man seized him roughly from behind, his huge forearms locked beneath Father Michel's chin. With the other hand he plunged the knife deeply between the priest's shoulder blades. As Father Michel gasped for breath the young man grasped his legs and, with a terrific jerk upwards, hurled him over the bridge and into the Seine. He leaned over the parapet, admiring his work.

'Who would have thought the old fool would make such a splash? A nice treat for the fishes this night!'

Then, looking about himself cautiously and observing a crowd emerging from a salon, he sloped off into the darkness.

Father Michel felt himself falling, falling like a stone, with biting coldness all around him and piercing through him. He struggled frantically but the black waters pressed upon him like a relentless smothering pillow. Still he fought and wrestled, thrashing about wildly, but he was borne down, borne inevitably down. In the black turmoil of suffocation he gasped, 'Marie, Mother of God. Marie, my love. Marie Gouze.'

Then his lungs filled like bellows and he uttered no more. The unconscious, drowning body rolled along the black, swirling waters. The body rolled along and was discovered the next morning, passive and inert, washed up on the banks of the Seine. A small crowd gathered around the sodden heap, it looked like a great, soaked, dead raven. They rolled the corpse over and one man stooped and wrenched from the neck a small crucifix, fashioned in gold. It was not worth much, to be sure, but the executioner was entitled to his perquisite.

November 1793 Execution

The trial of Olympe de Gouges was a great disappointment to the people of Paris who crowded into the public galleries. They had expected such amusement! Here was a woman who had had a great deal to say for herself, and now was her opportunity, for the services of a lawyer were not generally granted to prisoners of the revolution. She would have to speak for herself. Those who had read her posters, placarded through the streets of Paris — and there were hundreds who had — expected a fine tirade from this small virago with a past reputation as a courtesan and a present reputation for wit and false wisdom. What a comedown! They saw instead a small, shrunken woman, really she looked quite *old,* where was the accredited beauty? Her responses were quiet, lifeless, really she seemed indifferent to the whole proceedings. It was all sadly disappointing.

Marie stared unseeingly at the rows of curious faces. Slightly above her eye level, on the opposite wall, there was a large flaw in the plaster, a splayed out crack, like a spider's web. Really, she thought, it was very like a spider's web. She remembered the dew-spangled spiders' webs that used to be woven into the hedgerows that skirted the meadows of Pont d'Herault. Once, when she was a small child, she had reached her hand into the hedgerow, and, fascinated, twirled the delicate threads around her fingers. It had been unkind to the spider, she knew later, but life was unkind, cruel, to men, women and beasts. It was an indifferent Universe. But it did not seem to matter any more. She was weary of it.

The prosecutor droned on interminably. He was talking about a dangerous woman, *an enemy of the beloved leaders of our people.* It did not seem to be anything to do with her, so she scarcely listened.

Perhaps God and his world did exist, but if so, they had nothing to do with her. She was far away, shut out, as the farthest star is shut out from the light of the sun. She had planned, when Michel should next come, to make love with him, of course. But she would also tell him everything, all the great doubts she had withheld through the years. Her great fault had been her lack of faith, and she had never confessed it, for fear of losing his love. God had been held at a distance because she had been dishonest with herself, and with Michel, right back to the time when the first Holy Communion wafer had stuck in her throat, so many years ago. But it was eight weeks since his visit to her cell, and he had not come again. At the time when she most needed him, he had deserted her. After all, he was as other men. She would not live any longer in a life of fantasy. There was not much life left, after all, so it did not matter in the least. But *why had he not come?*

The prosecutor was banging on the table, demanding she speak. Wearily, for she was truly indifferent to the whole proceeding, she dragged her mind back to the present situation. The prosecutor was accusing her of slandering the peoples' friends, Robespierre and others, and insisting she reply. She sighed. 'My feelings have not changed. I regard them as self-seeking, ambitious men. I have said so many times. Why must there be this continual repetition of what everyone knows? I am weary of it and only beg you to hasten the end of this dreary affair.'

Really, it was all very poor sport! Fewer people turned out on the second day of the trial and by the third, when the sentence was to be pronounced, the room was half empty, for word had got around that Olympe de Gouges was nothing like the spitfire of old, quite a bore in fact. Before the sentence was read out she was asked, as was the custom, if she had anything to say. She was silent for a moment and then replied, expressionlessly,

'Yes, I have. As it happens, the court will be deprived of shedding my blood. I am pregnant and am going to give a citizen or citizeness to the republic.'

Here, at last was a sensation! Even at the height of the terror it was forbidden to send a pregnant woman to the guillotine. But as soon as she had spoken she regretted it, for the death sentence was pronounced, subject to a gynaecological examination.

'No!' she cried, animated at last. 'I will not submit to this indignity. It matters not, after all. I am ready to die, anyway. I am ready, I tell you!'

But they dragged her away, regardless of her protests, and two doctors and a midwife examined her that afternoon. As she lay naked, her limbs splayed apart while they poked and prodded her, she thought about the carcasses in the butchery at Montauban, stretched on the wooden slabs. It seemed a very long time ago. In her head she heard again the dull thud of the axe severing the calves' heads from their torsos. Would the guillotine sound like that, she wondered. At least, Father

Michel had assured her she would know nothing of the blood. She had that to thank him for.

They found no certain signs of pregnancy. Her age was against her — she was forty-five — and also her three months of imprisonment, though that was not necessarily conclusive. Everyone knew that snatched encounters were an everyday occurrence at L'Abbaye and besides, she had been a privileged private prisoner.

'It is possible, but unlikely, I should say,' said the midwife. 'She had her opportunities, to be sure, and more likely than not she took advantage of them. After all, she was a whore by trade, 'tis well known.'

'And not in bad shape for her age,' replied one of the doctors, squeezing a naked breast judiciously. 'Though, for myself, I prefer a plumper pigeon!'

So that was the end. She was bundled back into a cell to spend the last two days of her life. This was a different cell, much smaller and more confined than her previous quarters. In this one, lying on her back on the straw strewn floor, she could see the sky through a gap in the corner of the ceiling. There was nothing else to see, so she spent all her time watching the clouds and the slowly changing colours of the sky as day drifted into night. She waited and mused on the inconsequential nature of life, twisting straw around her fingers. It was very inconvenient that, longing for death as she had since Michel had not come to her, she yet still feared the guillotine. She was thinking of this little irony, looking at the sky, with one restless hand imprisoned behind her head, when, suddenly she was aware of the opening of the door, aware of another person in the room with her. She started up on her elbow, seeing out of the corner of her eye the black folds of a cassock sweeping the floor. For an infinitesimal moment she felt a surge of hope, then, seeing the face of a very old priest she had never in her life seen before, she sank back, crying pettishly, 'Go away! I do not require your services!'

Ignoring her, he sat down on a low stool and looked at her. He quietly stroked his fingers. His eyes were fixed on his fingers, long, sinewy fingers which reminded her of two little animals playing together. He sat still and silent for so long that she almost forgot that her was there. At last he spoke.

'Are you perhaps one who had turned away from the church in these troubled times, my dear? If so, I have been misinformed. I was told a priest came to see you several weeks ago. Thus, I imagined you might welcome the services of the church now your time on earth is so nearly at an end.'

'Do you know the priest who visited me?' she enquired eagerly.

'No, I do not know him. I come solely for the good of your soul in this time of extremity. It cannot matter which priest hears your last confession.'

'It can matter to me!' she cried, enraged. 'There was a priest who I loved better than God himself, but like God, he has betrayed my love. All my life I have been called a sinner. I have sinned in disliking and despising my husband, I have sinned in providing for the pleasures of men. I have sinned in caring about the evils of society. And, do you know, Father, there has always been a secret sin I have told no one. So hear it now. I have always felt the emptiness, the sheer nothingness of the church's sacrament. But, after all, what does it matter?'

'What you feel, my child, is despair. It is the gravest of all sins.'

She did not answer him. She had lived her life in a certain way. She had made choices, where she could have made others. And what did it all amount to? That, from the day she was born, she had been waiting for the morrow. She had been born that she might live until tomorrow, then it would be over. All the intensity of feeling, all the hopes and ideals and love she had felt would be razed to the ground in the single descent of a sharp blade. The strange thing was, it was the same for this man, this priest, for everyone. They were all condemned. The labour of ages, the inspiration of men and women, the brightest hopes for the future were all destined, ultimately, to perish in the conflagration of a universe in ruins. So, what did it matter that Father Michel had not returned? It was not worth a single thought, nor this conversation with an aged priest a single breath. She had little time, it was true. But she felt no despair. She felt free. So, at last she answered him.

'Do not, I beg of you, tell me what I feel or how to feel. I wish to spend the time I have left in solitude. Therefore, go.'

He did so, shaking his head like a dog worrying a bone, muttering of the poor woman's derangement. He opened his mouth to say he would pray for her, as he stood at the door, but the stony expression in her eyes made him change his mind.

Once the priest had gone, she became calm again. But the effort of ridding herself of him had tired her, so she lay back on the straw and was soon asleep. When she awoke she thought for a moment that she was in a meadow at Pont d'Herault, with the prickly grass tickling her neck. Smells of the countryside, remembered smells, seemed to drift through the opening in the ceiling, the cool night air fanned her cheeks.

Then she saw that the stars were shining down from a million miles away. Sighing with relief, she realised where she was. It was truly over. Rising, she began to dress, methodically. She must have slept for a long time. The night would soon be over and there was one task left to be done. She called the serving woman to bring her writing materials and, when they arrived, sat down to write a farewell letter to her son. Convention permitted a final letter, but she had no inclination to write to Father Michel. Her letter was quite short and perfunctory, why waste time on impassioned eloquence when all her writing had led her to this pitiful end?

I die, my son, a victim of my idolatry of my country and of the people. Their enemies, beneath the mask of republicanism, have led me remorselessly to the scaffold... Farewell, my son, when you receive this letter, I shall be no more.

Then she continued to dress with her accustomed care, not thinking of anything at all but the appearance she would make when the dawn came and they would escort her to the tumbril. Her efforts were rewarded. On her way to have her hair cut for the execution, a young man tossed a posy of violets to her. She sniffed them and smiled serenely. She glanced coquettishly at the young man as the tumbril rattled away.

1794 Pierre's Last Word

At last it is over, at last I am safe. The past few weeks and months have been an agony of worry and uncertainty as I have sought to extricate myself and my family from all association with my accursed mother. Now at last she is no more and I have her final letter to prove it. Assuredly, it completely failed to arouse any feelings of filial affection or sorrow for her fate. I predicted long ago that she would come to such an end. I have had to exercise great care and ingenuity, to be assured that I am not associated with her, despite being her son.

It was not difficult to bring her antics to the attention of the Committee for Public Safety. She drew too much attention to herself and they would have noticed her anyway, without my help. Nevertheless, I am quite proud of the part I played in her downfall. It took some shrewd political moves to make the acquaintance of Maximilien Robespierre. (My mother, for all her ranting and flourishing, had no political skill!) Actually, the acquaintance came about quite casually, to all appearances. I found out that Robespierre shared rooms in the *Rue Saintonge* and had the very odd habit of walking in the Tuileries Garden to feed the sparrows. Now, feeding the birds is something he would have had in common with my mother – the only thing! Paris was a hotbed of intrigue in those early years of the 1790s and there was plenty of opportunity to fraternize with the new leaders of France, although, quite frankly, things were in such a state of flux that the new leaders of one year were likely to be the headless corpses of the next. The important thing was to keep one's eyes and ears open – and to back the right horses.

Robespierre cut a strange figure, very dandified in appearance. He dressed very neatly, with his hair brushed and carefully powdered, but still, he had an odd look, mincing along on his high heels. He was too short, for one thing, and had a nasty greenish tinge to his skin. His face was pitted and pock-marked too, and he had a great bulging brow bone, altogether not a pretty sight. They say he was not much of a speaker, either, at the Committee for Public Safety, and that I can believe, for he did not look at me when I spoke to him, but answered in an irritatingly pompous voice. Still, he was interested in what I had to say. The great thing was, he had a reputation for being a woman-hater, which suited my purposes nicely.

I made it my business to saunter up to him in the Tuileries Gardens and told him where he would find the latest writings of Olympe de Gouges, not in her apartment, but in a warehouse where she stored her writings. The latest was an unfinished play called *La France Sauvee ou le Tyran Dethrone,* all about saving France and "reforming the monarchy". It depicts Marie Antoinette planning to retain the defamed monarchy and meeting the revolutionary forces, including one Olympe de Gouges herself. Then, if you can believe it, my besotted mother lectures the queen about her past behaviour and advises her about how to be a good republican leader! Such nonsense, but bound to inflame Robespierre, the mere idea of women seeing themselves as leaders! He was naturally incensed and more than ever determined that she would lose her head. I had every sympathy with his views, although, as I say, it did not really need my intervention to bring about her downfall.

My own position was precarious, of course. I was known as her son. Much good that cursed relationship has done for me! I was kept under surveillance during her imprisonment and trial, not myself imprisoned I am glad to say, for my freedom was necessary to carry out certain rather important tasks I needed to complete. One of them, of course, was to attend her execution. But I have to admit, it was a sad disappointment, a very tame affair. She looked very remote, very far away, as if she did not care. I tried desperately to catch her eye, I was determined to make her see me as the tumbril went past, but she did not look my way, she was smiling at some poor fool who threw her flowers. A courtesan's smile to the last! She did not even bother to speak from the scaffold, she who had spent so much of her life ranting and raving and interfering in the affairs of men! She simply forgave the executioner, as is the custom, and declared she was weary of the revolution, weary of her life and happy to die.

Then they executed her in the usual way. As I may have said, I rather enjoy the scene of the guillotine, the thud of the prisoner being thrown on the plank, then the next thud of the neck clamp being fixed. Then the swishing of the blade and the glorious flow of blood as the head falls. This time should have been rather special, but it was somehow rather an anticlimax. I felt, hollow, empty, rather as if something had died in me. Perhaps hatred had died. I cannot explain it.

Ten days after her execution, I was compelled to sign a "profession of civic faith", denying sympathy with my mother's views and professing my own patriotism to the new regime. Well, there was no compulsion really, for I have never shared her ridiculous convictions. The profession was nothing but the truth. Now I must prepare to leave France; there is no future for me here. I shall go to the colonies, to Guyana. It is not the future I expected when I embarked on a military career, but it may be a good life. Naturally, I shall take my wife and children with me. I shall sell my house and all my possessions, including my wife's jewelry. One small souvenir of these troubled times I may keep, a small gold crucifix I came by, not entirely by chance. I shall interest myself in trade in Guyana, and, with good fortune, will build a new life. But, assuredly, I shall pay no attention to my mother's views on the treatment of slaves. I never had any time for her opinions and it seems very clear to me that neither does anyone else.

Select Bibliography

Andress, D. (2005) *The Terror. Civil War and the French Revolution.* London, Abacus
Blanning, T.C.W. (1987) *The French Revolution. Aristocrats versus Bourgeois?* London, Macmillan
Burke, E. (1790) (2006 edn.) *Reflections on the Revolution in France.* Mineola, N.Y. Dover Publications
Caryle, T. (1837) (2002 edn.) *The French Revolution: A History.* N.Y. Modern Library
Cobban, A. (1963) *A History of Modern France. Vol 1: 1715-1799.* London, Penguin
Davidson, I. (2010) *Voltaire: A Life.* London, Profile Books
Hibbert, C. (1982) *The French Revolution.* London, Penguin
Kelly, L. (1989) *Women of the French Revolution.* London, Hamish Hamilton
Mousset, S. (2007) *Women's Rights and the French Revolution. A Biography of OLympe de Gouges.* New Brunswick, USA. Transaction Publishers
Rousseau, J.J. (1762) (1989 edn.) *Emile.* London, Everyman
Rude, G. (1964) *Revolutionary Europe 1783-1815.* London, Fontana
Voltaire (F.M.Arouet) *Candide.* (tr.Butt, J. 1947) London, Penguin
Voltaire (F.M.Arouet) *Lettres Philosophiques.* (tr.Tanock, L. 1980) London, Penguin